"Diana And I Are Getting Married."

Mac drew her closer to his side. "Did you all hear that?" he called out to the crowd.

A cheer went up from everybody.

"Mac, can we talk?" Diana asked weakly.

"Later, honey. They're judging the cook-off right now. And I want to be here to get *my* trophy."

Then a guilty expression crossed his face. "I was stuck. The marriage was a stroke of genius. I needed an edge to win— Donaldson's got some secret spice grown by his housekeeper. All I had was you," he whispered desperately.

"You—!"

"That's good. Let all that hostility come out," he said, looking around. "But not here."

Miss Simpson's voice crackled over the microphone. "We have this year's winner—Mac MacLean!"

Locking his fingers with Diana's, Mac pulled her toward the waiting judge. He raised his trophy in his free hand. "Thanks to my good-luck charm—my future wife, Diana."

He kissed her full on the lips, then whispered, "Don't worry. I've got everything under control."

Dear Reader:

I hope you've been enjoying 1989, our "Year of the Man" at Silhouette Desire. Every one of the twelve authors who are contributing a *Man of the Month* has created a very special someone for your reading pleasure. Each man is unique, and each author's style and characterization give you a different insight into her man's story.

From January to December, 1989 will be a twelve-month extravaganza spotlighting one book each month with special cover treatment as a tribute to the Silhouette Desire hero—our *Man of the Month*!

Created by your favorite authors, these men are utterly captivating—and I think Mr. June, Annette Broadrick's Quinn McNamara, will be simply... *Irresistible*! One of Lass Small's Lambert sisters gets a very special man in July. *Man of the Month* Graham Rawlins may start as the *Odd Man Out*, but that doesn't last long....

Yours,

Isabel Swift

Senior Editor & Editorial Coordinator

CAIT LONDON
The Loving Season

Silhouette Desire

Published by Silhouette Books New York

America's Publisher of Contemporary Romance

SILHOUETTE BOOKS
300 East 42nd St., New York, N.Y. 10017

ISBN: 0-373-05502-1

First Silhouette Books printing June 1989

Printed in the U.S.A.

CAIT LONDON

lives in the Missouri Ozarks but grew up in Washington and still loves craggy mountains and the Pacific coast. She's a full-time secretary, a history buff and an avid reader who knows her way around computers. She grew up painting—landscapes and wildlife—but is now committed to writing and enjoying her three creative daughters. Cait has big plans for her future—learning to fish, taking short trips for research and meeting people. She also writes as Cait Logan and has won *Romantic Times*'s Best New Romance Writer award for 1986.

For all the good guys,
with their tender hearts,
and especially for Donna

One

The whine of bagpipes floated on the frigid night wind as Diana walked toward the lights of a farmhouse. Located just off the deserted Colorado highway, the large two-story house loomed amid sprawling pastures. At eleven o'clock on Halloween night, the house looked as eerie and foreboding as Count Dracula's castle. The surrounding buildings looked capable of holding a crowd of zombies each, and the weathered barn seemed the perfect hiding place for a mummy.

"A mix-up in reservation," she muttered. She glanced back at her station wagon parked at the gate to the MacLean ranch. Nestled in the shadows of a tall aspen, the car looked safer than she felt.

The Rayfield Inn clerk had thoroughly apologized for mistakenly placing her reservation for December.

"Sure am sorry, lady. We're booked up solid this week. But let me make a call—Old Mac puts up our leftovers once in a while. It's miles to the next town, and chances are they're booked up, too. It's hunting season, you know."

Diana glanced at the rugged San Juan mountains, silhouetted against the clear night sky. A gust of icy wind swept up her neck, whipping her short hair about her face. The cold air penetrated her green sweater and blue jeans, and she shivered. Stuffing her freezing hands into the pockets of her denim jacket, she wondered who slept in her nice warm room in the inn.

Diana had wanted quiet and time to weigh her life and her future, and the travel brochure for Benevolence's only bed-and-breakfast inn had made the tiny town seem ideal. Situated up in the mountains and overlooking the upper Rio Grande river, Benevolence had been deserted by miners at the turn of the century and now catered to those who craved fresh air and majestic scenery.

I'm a forty-two-year-old orphan, she thought darkly. Twenty years as a housewife and supportive mate had ended with the crushing discovery of her husband, Alex's, frequent infidelity. She had scrambled out of the marriage with as much sanity and dignity as she could manage. When the divorce was final, her fears had eased a little. With careful managing, she could save enough of the child support allotments to provide for her two sons' future college expenses.

Having no employable skills had left her confidence shaken and her financial survival questionable. But she'd snagged a job that offered a small paycheck *and* a training period. Teaching clients how to run several different software programs began as part-time work, then bloomed into a well-paying learning experience. Taking a deep breath, Diana had waded through selling the huge family house, giving Alex his half and buying a modest, more practical home.

Diana had run on nothing but the will to survive, each day testing her mental and physical abilities. Finally the day came when she realized how utterly dry she felt inside. She'd taken a hard look at her modest savings, and with the instincts of a bird let out of a cage, she'd decided to fly.

Quitting her job had been difficult, but the manager was also a divorcée, and she had understood. With Rick and Blaine both away at college, Diana leased her home for a year and packed the bare necessities into her car. For the first time, she was going to find what she really wanted out of her life. Reserving a room for a week was her first step. She'd worry about the second step after resting; she'd earned that privilege, after all.

Now, two years after the divorce, Diana—out on her own at last—was a bed-and-breakfast "leftover."

"Okay, Diana, admit it," she coached herself as she had in the recent past. "You're tired and you're cold and you're peeved about some blasted hunter snoring in your room. Part of being an independent woman is recognizing what you feel."

Her mouth tightened as a wave of bitterness swept over her. But then, divorce did that to a person, she decided. It left sharp edges.

As she neared the white farmhouse, she heard the sound of a dog howling to the music of the bagpipes. Hereford cattle stirred in the barn lot, lowing as she passed. A bulky shadow swayed beside the fence, and Diana stopped to stare at a large buffalo.

Taking a deep breath, she hurried to the house, marched up the wooden steps and across the wide porch to the front door. "Whoever is playing that...instrument, needs lessons," she muttered as she jabbed at the doorbell.

The shrill sound of the ancient buzzer caused her to jump back. Instantly the bagpipes stilled and a dog began barking excitedly. Oh, great, Diana thought, reminded of the sharp teeth of the Hound of the Baskervilles.

The porch light snapped on, and she blinked, surprised. The door opened, and the fiercest man she had ever seen stepped out, thrusting an overflowing bowl of candy at her. Dressed in an open flannel shirt and worn jeans, he glared down at her from his six-foot-plus height. The wind whipped his slightly long dark hair around his face. Bagpipes were tucked under his arm, wheezing their last throes. "A little old for trick-or-treating, aren't you?" he asked in a voice that made her think of a grizzly bear disturbed while hibernating.

She tilted her head back to stare at his very dark eyes. She didn't like his imperious tone, not a bit. Alex had used it too many times—whenever he'd told her what to do. Right now, she felt bone-tired and was in no mood for a dominating male. "I am not trick-or-treating."

Before she could continue, a massive husky ran out of the house and stopped before her. Legs wide apart and hackles raised, it regarded her closely. Diana decided it was male when it growled at her, baring huge teeth. His protectiveness seemed to her to be unnecessary, considering how tall and muscular his master was.

They were a matched set, Diana thought. Two males disturbed in their castle, defending their territory from an encroaching female.

"Quiet, Red," the man ordered roughly. The dog calmed instantly. "Car trouble, then," the man snapped, turning to look at the road that led to his ranch. "Women. They should stay home where they belong."

He glanced down at the husky, who was padding around Diana's legs, sniffing her curiously. "Red isn't used to perfume," he explained. "Get back, Red."

Diana could feel the cords in her neck tighten with anger at the man's arrogance. She hadn't driven practically nonstop from Missouri just to be at the mercy of someone who shared her ex-husband's chauvinistic views!

"What's the problem? Radiator? Run out of gas?" he rattled off as he placed the candy dish back inside the house.

Diana took a deep breath, trying to rein in the temper she'd discovered she had during the divorce. "The Rayfield Inn sent me," she stated through gritted teeth. "The clerk called?"

He answered with a nod. His eyes ran down her petite body, lingering on the curves. "I didn't know Ray would send me a woman." He took a deep weary breath, as though he'd baby-sat every woman from Colorado to Wyoming and was deeply tired of the entire female race.

His jaw, too square for him to be handsome, jutted out pugnaciously. "I'm fixing chili for a cook-off tomorrow. I don't have time to make you comfortable. You'll have to do that yourself. Get in here."

Diana's temper began to send out big red warning flares. Caveman-style hospitality, she thought. "I wouldn't think of disturbing you," she stated icily. "After meeting you, I really don't think this is a very good idea, after all."

The man's bushy brows rose. "Well now, spitfire, don't go getting snooty. If you're looking for a bed, it's my house or Wyoming."

She glared up at him, all six-foot-plus of male superiority. She'd rather freeze to death on the Colorado mesas than ask him for help. "I'm so sorry I interrupted your symphony. Thank you for the invitation, but no thanks."

"If you're thinking about sleeping in your car, forget it. It's damned cold and dangerous for a little thing like you."

Diana took a deep breath, counting silently to ten to steady her rising anger. "I am quite able to take care of myself, Mr. MacLean."

She pivoted, took one step and felt his big hand latch on to her belt. He pulled her into his house as easily as if she were a child.

Diana's carefully checked temper erupted. The door clicked shut just as her open hand met his hard cheek. "How dare you?" she exclaimed, stepping back. Her anger swept over her like a Colorado forest fire fanned by a high wind.

He tossed the bagpipes to a battered couch. His eyes blazed. "Lady, I dare plenty when some half-grown female thinks she can take me on."

His mouth tightened into a grim line, and he looked at her from head to toe. His hard gaze seemed to penetrate her thick winter clothes and note her thinness underneath. "You barely outweigh Red. You don't look like you've got enough fight left in you to start anything."

Pride kept Diana from rubbing her burning palm. She still felt the pain of contact right up to her shoulder. Stunned, she realized she'd never hit another person in her life. She felt her knees go weak and her skin prickle. Why in heaven's name had she slapped him? He was so big, she barely reached his shoulder. "Keep your hands off me," she warned, spacing the words carefully.

"You're nothing but skin and bone. When I put my hands on a woman, I like something soft and warm."

Diana glared at the hardest face she had ever seen. Lines crossed his forehead, creasing the deeply tanned skin. His hair was as black as midnight but shot by streaks of white at the temples. His deep-set eyes glittered menacingly above prominent cheekbones. But when he scratched his muscular chest, which was covered by dark hair, she felt something within her stir.

He pointed at the telephone, almost buried under a stack of sportsmen's magazines. "There's the phone. Find someplace else, if you can. Good luck."

He turned and walked off, presenting Diana with a view of his broad back. She allowed her eyes to wander down to his lean hips and long legs, then to his feet. He wore a red sock and a green sock. Both heels were worn through.

Diana took a deep breath and hugged herself. Uneasy, she glanced away from the tattered hole on his jeans, which revealed the back of his muscular thigh. Maybe he needed money.

The husky stared up at her. "Shoo!" Diana whispered. "Go away."

He growled ominously just as a large white cat strolled into the room. While the cat twisted around and rubbed against Diana's ankles, the massive dog seemed to wither. He stared warily at the feline as he backed away a foot.

When the cat began to walk, tail held high, toward the dog, the beast fled after his master as though his life were in danger.

"Nice kitty. Stay here, kitty," Diana cooed. "I bet you're female." She drew the inn's telephone number from her pocket and dialed. After five rings, a sleepy voice answered, "Rayfield Inn."

When Diana explained that "Old Mac" wasn't exactly hospitable and asked for other recommendations, the clerk chuckled. "Nope. None. You'll have to make do."

"'Mac is a good old boy,'" she intoned, repeating the clerk's description as she hung up.

"I can't imagine staying a night, let alone a week," Diana muttered, glancing around at the battered furniture. Huge hunting bows and quivers of arrows hung on the oak paneling. A cabinet of assorted rifles stood in a disheveled corner. A variety of tattered scatter rugs covered the worn carpeting. Beneath a curtainless window, a sheet covered an angular object.

She picked up a magazine designed for cattlemen and read the address label: Mac MacLean, Rural Route, Benevolence, Colorado. She closed her eyes, thinking of her modest home in southwest Missouri—her safe home, free from black-eyed giants and bagpipes.

But Missouri also held painful memories and friends torn between Alex and herself. She had launched this trip with a desperate determination to slug it out with her past and find her future, to meet herself as a woman. She had to survive. *She had to.*

A ripple of sheer fatigue almost sent her to the overstuffed couch. Oh, how she'd love to crawl under that crocheted afghan and sleep.

The toe of her left sneaker touched something, and she glanced down. Mac MacLean's work-worn boots reminded her of the man's ungroomed appearance.

Tossing the magazine onto the cluttered coffee table, she glanced longingly at the huge black wood-burning stove placed against one wall. A blazing fire crackled and lured her a step nearer. "I'd be safer in the station wagon, freezing. No telling what type of person this MacLean is."

Mac didn't need any half-pint female making him feel like a heel, he decided as he stalked back into the living room. He jammed his fists on his waist and faced her, not bothering to temper his belligerence. "This chili cook-off is important to me. Last year Fred Donaldson won, but this year I want the trophy. Got it?" He scowled at her. "It takes all night to make my chili recipe. Can't leave it for a minute. Did you find a place to stay?"

Looking at her big brown eyes, Mac felt himself go all weak. Who would she call? She had a stranded look about her, and there was something so soft about her pale face that touched him.

She'd slapped him hard, but Mac had seen the undeniable fear widen her eyes...as though she had expected him to return the blow. He'd seen enough of the wounded to recognize this woman as a refugee from pain.

"What's your name?" he asked roughly, to cover the emotions churning within him. The woman looked as though she were glued together by sheer determination and not much else, but he had to admit she had plenty of spirit. Right now, she stood ramrod straight, her eyes meeting his defiantly.

"Diana Phillips," she answered.

Mac liked the low wispy sound of her voice. It reminded him of the mountain wind sweeping through pine needles. He stared at her curiously. She had a classy look, he decided, wondering suddenly how many women would look as good without makeup. Her short dark brown hair glistened beneath the overhead light. Her lips, although pressed together firmly, still showed their soft full shape. But it was her eyes that tore at him. They were so wary beneath layers of long straight black lashes.

She looked like a stray, Mac decided finally. And he had always taken care of strays.

"Diana," he repeated gently, watching her small teeth tug at her bottom lip. "Di."

For just a second, her brown eyes turned almost black. "I detest that name, Mr. MacLean," she declared passionately. "I'm a little old for nicknames."

"Diana," he said carefully, meeting her on her own territory. "You're wearing a big chip on that little shoulder."

She glared at him for just a second, then turned her head to look out at the cold night. She's skittery as a colt, Mac thought. The urge to pick her up and hold her was so strong he took a step toward her. He saw her small body tense. "I'll take care of you," he whispered huskily. He was glad then that he ran his ranch with the help of neighbors and highschool boys. With no one else around, he was the only one available to help her.

He'd ached for a woman's pain before, had held her as her life slipped away... He swallowed hard, forcing the past behind him.

Diana looked up at him. "I don't need your help, Mr. MacLean."

What the hell, Mac decided instantly. He had the extra room; it wouldn't matter if he took a few minutes to make her comfortable. The chili cook-off was important to him, but he'd lost to Donaldson before. Diana needed him now, and he wasn't letting her escape into the cold night.

Appointing himself her protector, Mac crossed his arms in front of his chest. Every woman deserved her white knight, and he decided to be Diana's.

"I must be going, Mr. MacLean. Thank you for the telephone."

She'd walk out his door if he didn't act soon. "Call me Mac, but skip the MacLean," he ordered gently. "Look, I've been thinking. If you'll follow my directions *exactly*, I'll let you finish browning the meat for my chili. While you're doing that, I'll clear out the spare room and get your things from the car."

She hesitated. "I'm not a cook, Mr.—"

"Mac—most people call me Mac." He could feel her trying to get away from him. And he couldn't allow that. Strays often hurt themselves, and he was certain that would happen to her; she looked as if she bore the weight of the world on her shoulders.

"Listen. I've cut my own prime beefsteak just right for chili. It's browning in the skillet now. All you have to do is stir it up once in a while."

"No," she repeated sharply, buttoning up her jacket to the neck. "I need a room, not sympathy. But thank you for the offer."

Then he knew. She was damned independent and wouldn't give an inch unless she could give him something substantial back.

Frustrated, he pushed his fingers through his hair. "Okay, then what about cleaning up the kitchen and the spare room . . . when you're rested?"

When he caught the flicker of interest in her eyes, he continued, "What I said about clearing the room out, I meant. I've been using it for storage. You can change the sheets and whatnot."

"What about your chili?"

"It'll keep." Mac didn't hesitate; he had snared her, and he intended to keep her safe, if only for the night.

He sat and put on his boots. Standing up, he saw Diana taking in the length of him. He'd never seen such wounded eyes on a grown woman. How old was she? Twenty? Thirty-five?

"That's right. I'm a big hombre—it runs in the family," he murmured gently. He reached out his hand slowly, taking care not to alarm her. "I'll need your keys. You can hold my house for ransom."

"I can bring my bags in myself...if I decide to stay."

"I've got the room, and I could use some help cleaning up." Testing her, he held his hand steady, palm up. Come on, he coaxed her silently. You have to trust someone.

She stared at him, trying to read his expression, then carefully extracted her keys from her jeans. She dropped them into his palm, and he noted the slender pale hands with their perfect nails. Soft hands, he thought....

Shoot. He always was a pushover where strays were concerned.

He grabbed his shearling coat and called for Red. Walking out the door, he said, "See you in a little bit." He needed the brisk walk in the cold air to think.

Outside, the frigid wind chilled his nostrils and throat as he remembered her tense face. He scowled. Was she married?

He decided then to keep her—if he could.

"Keep her," he murmured, slightly surprised at his thoughts. He chuckled. It was ridiculous. This woman couldn't be added to his menagerie. Diana didn't fit in with the owls with broken wings and the motherless fawn. True, he wanted to hold her and protect her, as he did with the hurt animals he'd found. Then he remembered the curves beneath her clothes....

He shook his head to clear it. "Oh hell, she needs help, that's all."

He drove her white station wagon, coated with road dirt, to the house and brought her luggage in. Tucking Diana beneath his wing might take some doing because of her independent streak. But she'd trusted him with her keys, and that was a first step.

He had to keep her, somehow.

Diana took a deep breath and walked into Mac's kitchen. She would not owe him . . . or any man, ever.

She rubbed her palm against her thigh, remembering the hard slap. She closed her eyes. She'd never raised her hand in anger to anyone. Yet tonight, she'd let her buried fury explode against a stranger? Her reaction had been savage, impulsive. But then, Mac MacLean had the look of the untamed.

She took off her jacket and tossed it over an aged wooden chair. Rolling up her sweater sleeves, she surveyed the disaster. The old enamel sink had seen better days and was filled with an assortment of battered pots and dishes. An apartment-size electric stove, heaped with another stack of pans, stood in one corner. An ancient wood stove dominated the small kitchen. Shiny and black, trimmed with white enamel, the antique held a blazing fire.

On the table, Mac had carefully lined up his spices and cans of tomatoes. Diced onions and garlic were scattered across a wooden block. A scrubbed stockpot, filled with cooked red beans, stood next to a huge black skillet. Apparently, between blowing his bagpipe at odd hours and handing out candy, Mac had been carefully cooking his prizewinning chili.

Diana glanced at the iron skillet and knew that only a man the size of Mac could possibly lift it with one hand. She thought of his size, of the dark hair swirling over his broad chest, and shivered.

There was something about Mac that she responded to, and that frightened her deeply. She'd lost twenty years. What were the rules of the man-woman game now?

Diana stared into the night beyond the kitchen window. Wide-eyed and innocent at twenty, she had married Alex with all the bright hopes of a bride. Painful memories now wrapped around her, and Diana heard an anguished sob that was her own.

She had to survive—to place the pain behind her and seek the flow of the rest of her life.

The cat rubbed against her legs, and Diana reached down to scratch her ears. "I like you, kid. Stay by me when that monster of a dog comes back, will you?"

The animal purred and rubbed harder, then jumped onto a chair and looked at her with unblinking yellow eyes.

Taking a deep breath, Diana began searching for the dishwashing detergent, plugged the sink with the rubber stopper and turned on the faucets. Great, she thought, testing the water—cold water.

Knowing about old stoves, Diana lifted a lid and discovered the hot water reserve. She dipped a clean pot into it, filled the sink and began washing the dishes.

She heard the car door slam, then Mac's movements as he went about preparing the spare room for her. There was something companionable about the sounds, she decided, scraping the burnt film from a pan.

Diana knew how to clean with a fury. She'd done it endless times.

She grimaced, scrubbing a battered pot with a scouring pad. She'd read an article once about the compulsive need to clean. The endless urge, according to the author, was fueled by the need to fill an emotional void.

Why hadn't she been enough?

Diana worked harder, feeling an almost frantic energy beat through her. She heard a slight noise and turned to see Mac watching her intently, his arms filled with chopped wood.

Something sizzled when their eyes met, and Diana felt an unwelcome flutter in her pulse. She lowered her gaze and scrubbed the pot harder. "I'm almost finished."

"I didn't ask you to wash the whole house. The cleaning up could have waited until you were rested," Mac murmured softly, dropping the wood into a box by the stove. He glanced at the pot in her shaking hands. "If you don't stop worrying that, you'll scrub a hole clean through it."

Realizing he was right, Diana stopped and rinsed and dried the remaining dishes, instead, stacking them carefully on the cabinet shelves.

Mac stripped off his coat, tossed it onto a wooden chair and sat. He began drawing off his boots. "I changed the sheets on the bed. Your keys and bags are on it."

"Thank you. I'll leave in the morning."

His bushy brows met in a scowl. "Why? I thought you needed a room for a week."

Diana's defenses rose. She felt her plans were being threatened by this man, felt him challenging her right to make her own decisions. "I can't stay."

"Like hell," he stated tersely. "We'll talk about this when you've had some rest."

"That sounds patronizing. As though I'm a sleepy grumpy child who can't think straight." Meek Diana Phillips, who never challenged anyone, suddenly wanted to tear into the arrogant Mac and read him her Bill of Rights. He might be a Colorado cattle baron, but he wasn't her lord and master.

While she simmered in her own juices, Mac thoughtfully rubbed his bearded jaw with his hand. The scraping sound caused her backbone to tingle.

"Can we talk about this some other time?" he asked in a reasonable tone. "I'm going to be busy with my chili all night."

"I don't see how that would change things. I wanted a vacation in a bed-and-breakfast and—"

"Stay here. What's the difference? I've got plenty of room." Mac shifted his large frame uneasily on the creaky wooden chair, glancing away from her like a boy caught in an act of mischief.

Diana watched the changing expression on his face and noted the fatigue deepening the lines around his eyes and mouth. "Why?"

He swallowed, stretching his long legs out to examine the mismatched socks on his feet. "I could say, nothing's open in Benevolence. But the truth is, I just want you here." Where you're safe, he added silently.

The simple statement jolted Diana to her fingertips, almost causing her to drop the chipped plate in her hands.

Mac glanced at her, scowling. "Be straight with a woman and you scare the wind out of her. Shoot. I've never been good at playing games.... Okay, I need the money. How about that one?''

She thought about the well-fed cattle and the sprawling land, and she knew that money was something that Mac did *not* need. Why did he want her to stay? ''Try again, Mac,'' she said quietly, watching him. ''I'm not buying that one.''

''Don't look so damned scared—you're white as a sheet.''

''I can't stay,'' she managed to say shakily, trying unsuccessfully to get her legs to walk toward the door. Everything south of her brain had apparently stopped functioning. Except for her heart, which was beating wildly.

At forty-two, Diana had never been alone in a house with any man other than her sons or her ex-husband. *She didn't know the rules of the game.*

''I can't,'' she repeated, fighting to draw air into her lungs.

''Why not?'' Mac asked curiously as he stood, moving closer to her, causing her throat to dry. ''Why are you so scared?'' he asked in a low tone that raised goose bumps all over her flesh. ''What have I done, Diana?''

The heat of his body penetrated her clothing, and Diana sidled a few inches away from him. Her hips met the kitchen counter, and she looked up at Mac's heavy frown.

He moved too quickly for her to escape the light sweep of his finger down her cheek. His eyes held hers with their gentleness. ''Since there isn't anyone else here to tell you this, I have to. I've never hurt a woman in my entire life. I like kids and I pay my bills. All in all, most women like me and trust me. You're the only one to slap me since I was a teenager.''

With a crooked grin, he added, ''Maybe I'm just lonesome tonight. You can move on in the morning if you want. But tonight, would you stay with me? Help me stir the chili, maybe have a cup of coffee? Or maybe we could play a game of cards and shoot some pool.''

The low wistful tone of his voice soothed Diana's worn nerves. She felt the taut wires within her loosen, the trembling of her fingers against the counter ease. His body heated hers and she felt herself almost lean toward him. Alex had never considered her as a companion, not for a moment.

Mac looked safe. Maybe, just for tonight. ''People would talk—your neighbors...''

His grin widened and Diana felt a wave of femininity wash over her.

''Shoot. I'm a big boy. Do you like poker or rummy?''

Diana smiled, realizing she'd just broken one of the chains to her past. She'd been cautious all her life. What would people think? had been her guideline for years. ''I would really like a cup of tea, Mac,'' she said softly, watching his eyes widen with surprise. ''If you have any tea, I'll make a pot.''

''Tea?'' he repeated blankly.

''Dried, crushed leaves,'' she explained, astonished at the teasing tone in her voice. ''You pour hot water over them and let them steep.''

''Uh-huh,'' he murmured, looking thoughtfully at the cupboards. He began jerking open doors and rummaging through the stuffed shelves. "I used to like the stuff. Drank gallons while I was waiting—"

"Waiting for what, Mac?" Diana asked when he didn't finish.

He pulled out a tin, lifting it like a prize. His eyes met hers, and she saw the ache there. "Waiting for my wife to die."

Just then, just for an instant, Diana wanted to move into his arms. The emotion was so strong that she took a step forward. To stop herself, she wrapped her arms around her chest and stared at the worn linoleum floor.

She was just tired and susceptible, she decided, watching Mac search the cupboards again to extract a delicate China teapot. He placed it on the table like a trophy, pushing aside his chili condiments. "There. I knew there was one around here somewhere," he stated proudly. He shoved the tin at her. "You'd better make it. When I make coffee, it tastes like mud. No telling what my tea would taste like now."

In the next hour, Diana experienced her first taste of a man's companionship.

She liked Mac and his concerned questions. "Do you think the tea is too old? Don't drink it if you don't like it."

The man needed company, and maybe she did, too. Just for one night. . . .

Sometime between his "Are you cold? I'll stoke up the stove," and watching him brown the meat for his chili, Diana's lids began to droop.

"Hey, Diana, do you know anything about chili?" Mac turned just as Diana fought to open her lids.

She smiled at him drowsily. "Mmm?"

Mac crouched in front of her, looking at her almost tenderly. "You're tired. Go on, the bedroom is just off the living room."

Diana yawned and stretched.

"Think about it after you've rested," Mac said, gently placing his hand on her knee. The vibrant warmth of his touch startled her, and a warning stirred within her. She moved her leg away.

How long had it been since she really trusted a man? What did Mac really want from her? Her head hurt with the questions racing through her brain. "I think I will go on to bed, if you don't mind."

"I'm not the kind to offer and not mean it," he snapped, offended. His broad shoulders tensed beneath the flannel shirt. "The bathroom isn't much, but there's clean towels."

Feeling Mac's curious gaze on her back, Diana left the kitchen and went into the small neat bedroom. He had turned back the patchwork quilt on the single bed; the tiny pink rosebuds decorating the sheets and pillows seemed to invite her...

Suddenly, Diana felt the weight of every mile from Missouri to Colorado in her bones and muscles. Without a second thought, she eased her bags to the floor, kicked off her shoes, then curled up in bed.

A moment later, she heard Mac's off-key singing. It soothed her torn nerves somehow, and she drifted off to sleep.

Two

Shhh, honey," Mac murmured, drawing the woolen afghan higher on Diana's shoulders.

Mac had opened the bedroom door to let the heat from the living room penetrate the cold room. Unable to keep himself from entering the room to make sure she was all right, he had stepped up to the bed and had become intrigued by how vulnerable she looked sleeping.

Honey. He'd used the word to comfort his wife, Eleanor. He'd grieved long and hard, and he didn't intend to open himself to that pain again.

With a fleeting sense of panic, he realized that Diana just might reopen his old wounds. He remembered the slender knee beneath his hand before she moved away.... He released the afghan, as though it burned his fingers.

He didn't need any stirring up at his age. He'd dealt with the pain, and he intended to keep his troubled waters smooth. Diana was hurting, and he just wanted to help, that's all, he rationalized.

"If there's one thing I know about myself, Red," he whispered to the dog, who had padded into the room, "I'm a sucker for anything that looks as though it needs tucking under my wing."

Diana slept heavily, oblivious to Mattie, the cat, who'd jumped up on the bed. Diana snuggled to the animal, and Mac decided to let Mattie stay there.

Mac had spent hours sitting at his wife's bedside, and now it seemed natural for him to settle into the old cherry rocker by the bed. Eleanor couldn't be healed, and he'd watched her seep into death, a part of him dying with her.

He realized he'd been thinking of Diana as "his stray" and quietly discussed her with Red. "She looked like a shivering kitten standing on the porch, cold but too proud to ask for a warm saucer of milk. Whether Ms. Diana Phillips will admit it or not, Red, she's hurting bad."

Diana shifted slowly, sighing tiredly.

He hadn't turned on the shortwave radio in his living room, not needing the chatter to fill his loneliness tonight—he had Diana. She looked small and just about the most feminine woman Mac had ever seen.

He picked up one of her shoes. It almost fit into the palm of his hand. Barely worn, the shoe was as new as her jeans and jacket. "Our Ms. Diana is on the run, Red," Mac murmured, leaning forward to lift a strand of red-brown hair back from her cheek. "She's scared of men."

Her skin enticed him. Smooth and pale, its fragrance wafted out to him, tantalizing him. Mac held his body rigid. How he wanted to hold her against him, just to comfort her.

All strays needed comforting, didn't they?

He wrapped his fingers around his knee to steady their trembling. Closing his eyes, he saw Eleanor's perfumes and powders discarded into the trash after her death. He shuddered, feeling a fresh streak of pain.

He smiled grimly, opening his lids. "Watch it, old man, you're having an off night. And an attack of the middle-age lonelies."

Patting Red's shaggy head, Mac continued his quiet monologue. "Halloween night and she strolls right in here. She's hunting something. . . . What is it?"

He studied Diana's face, the long lashes and the dark circles beneath her eyes. "She's exhausted, on the run and needing to hole up for a time. We can give her some peace, Red. If just for a short time."

Would she stay?

Diana's lashes fluttered and her eyes, glazed with sleep opened suddenly. She watched him warily. "Are you frightened of me, Diana?" he asked gently.

Her lids drifted down drowsily as she turned her back to him, drawing the afghan over her shoulder. "No."

Mac leaned forward, bracing his forearms over his knees. "Diana?"

"Mmm?"

"Diana, you're safe here. I'll take care of you."

"Mmm. That's good," she answered sleepily.

Mac settled back in the rocker to search out all the ways he could keep her near. By dawn he'd decided that sometimes strays needed to be lassoed and placed in a nice safe corral. Sometimes a cowboy had to move in quick and close the gate.

"Hey, sleepyhead, wake up," a masculine voice rumbled in Diana's ear. "Come on, wake up. Your breakfast is ready."

Keeping her lids closed, Diana relished the warmth that enveloped her. Then she heard a purr and felt a movement against her side. She also felt something heavy weighing down her legs. She quickly opened her eyes and found herself looking down at Red's dark brown eyes. She turned her head and saw the cat sleeping beside her.

"It's nine o'clock," the male voice continued softly. She felt a gentle hand stroking back the strand of hair clinging to her cheek. "You've slept almost nine hours."

Diana summoned her courage and looked into Mac's smiling eyes. He was sitting in the battered old rocker in front of the window. His jaw had grown a heavy beard during the night, and his hair was damp, clinging to his forehead. He'd obviously just showered. His deeply tanned chest was bare, and her fingers itched to play with the thick dark hair covering the muscular planes. She could almost feel the rough texture beneath her fingertips.

She swallowed and looked away, embarrassed by the flow of her thoughts. She blamed the early morning hours for her weakness. It still came hard—the sleeping alone.

Sensuality had never been a big part of her life with Alex, but for some reason, Mac made her feel conscious of herself as a woman.

She looked back at him when he chuckled. "I must be an unholy sight for a lady like you, Diana."

Gazing at her closely, he stopped smiling. "You're pretty first thing in the morning," he whispered huskily.

When Diana flushed, Mac stood to his full awesome height. "I'm not used to women waking up in the house. I'll shave and put on a shirt. Otherwise, you might slap me again for poor manners," he said, then turned and walked toward the kitchen.

She yawned and stretched, staring at Mac's back. It was a nice back, power evident in the muscles beneath the dark skin. By the rigid way he moved, she knew she'd hurt him. Mac couldn't understand how terrified she was of her emotions.

She sat up and dislodged the cat. Reluctantly leaving her warm nest, she moved to the windows, looking out at the heavy fog that covered the ranch. The cat rubbed against her legs, and she picked it up, taking it into the kitchen with her.

Mac had thrown on a green wool shirt, and standing in his bare feet before a mirror on the wall, was lathering his jaw with a foaming brush. He picked up an old-fashioned straightedge razor and saw her. "Sit down and eat. My coffee may not be any good, but I make the best pancakes in the country. Then we're going to the cook-off. Donaldson's chili hasn't got a chance this year."

Diana took a deep breath and hugged the purring cat, gathering her courage. "Mac, I'm not going with you. I'll freshen up, then be on my way."

He grinned. "Cranky little cuss in the morning, aren't you, Diana?"

She felt the slightest twinge of anger. Mac was trying to make her smile, but she didn't feel like smiling just yet. "I don't like being treated like a child, with you deciding where I'm going or what I'll be doing. A chili contest is not on my agenda."

He shifted on those incredibly long legs, turning toward her. His stance indicated that he would discuss the situation with her until she agreed. One of his heavy eyebrows rose. "No reason to balk, Diana. The cook-off is one of the kickoff festivities for the annual Benevolence Fall Hunt. The tourists like it. So do the hunters. Just part of the local color."

Diana put the cat on the floor and straightened up, uncomfortable with his friendly tone. Actually, she would like playing tourist, for a change of pace. But she could do so on her own.

Watching her mutinous expression, Mac's eyes narrowed. He moved his mouth to one side and took a clean swipe with the flashing blade. "Lady, I've got a hunch you could be trouble—real trouble," he mumbled, then took another swipe down his jaw. "You're too edgy and you've got a nasty right hook."

She glared at him, wanting to forget the slap. What right had he to go probing at her psyche, tearing at her privacy and taunting her? "You're just plain nasty," she flung back. "Bagpipes in the middle of the night," she scolded, feeling herself gear up. "You probably scare the poor bears out of their caves."

Mac's prominent chin jutted out beneath the shaving foam; a tiny white fleck clung to his ear. "Huh! Well, little lady, people around here ask me to play the bagpipes."

He pinched his nose, raising it to safety as he took another swipe with the razor. "Women," he muttered to the mirror. "You take 'em in, get 'em warm, and they turn on you the first chance they get."

"What did you say, Mac?" Diana asked. She watched his hand swish the razor in a small enamel basin. He dried the blade on a towel.

He pivoted, meeting her stare with his own. The opened shirt revealed that intriguing mass of hair covering his chest. "I said, it's a small thing, but it's important to me. I want you to go to the cook-off with me. Be my date, sort of. So far as I can see, there's no reason you can't come. Unless some jealous husband is going to come after my scalp."

"You don't need to worry—I'm divorced." His accusation had come quickly and too sharply, but somehow she thought he already knew about her.

Mac continued to look at her, and Diana could feel his challenge wrap around her. Long ago she'd stopped thinking of herself as a desirable woman, but now this rough-hewn cowboy was raising those emotions she had sheltered for an eternity. "I can't," she said weakly.

"Why in Sam Hill can't you?" he demanded, walking over to her. "Look, I checked back with Ray. You did have reservations for a full week. So you had plans to stay in Benevolence, anyway. Your room is gone, Diana. Ray rented it out to hunters from Missouri. There's snow coming down in the passes, and that little wagon of yours needs some fine-tuning. So what's your big excuse?''

Feeling flustered and feminine and utterly vulnerable, Diana shivered. In a gesture of self-protection, she wrapped her arms around herself. ''I don't owe you any explanation.''

''Huh!'' Mac snorted as he padded back to the mirror to complete his shaving. ''You don't have any reason not to spend the day with me, do you?''

''Maybe I just don't want to,'' Diana ventured softly, resenting how easily Mac had reduced her to sounding obstinate. ''You are a pushy man, Mac.''

''Pushy?'' he growled, taking out a pair of socks from his shirt pocket. She noted that one was navy blue and the other was black with red stripes. ''Nobody ever called me that before.''

''Then maybe it's time someone did.'' Diana badly needed the coffee he had offered. She reached for the battered tin pot on the stove.

''Use a pot holder,'' he warned behind her. ''I don't want you burning your hands.''

Taking a deep breath, Diana swiped a rag from the table and reached for a mug. ''I have been taking care of myself for quite a while now,'' she said through her teeth.

''I'll have a cup, please,'' Mac murmured near her. ''Maybe after we eat, both our temperaments will have improved.''

She glared at him, certain that nothing would improve her mood at the moment.

The poacher on her right grinned at her boyishly as he sat at the table. ''Okay, maybe I didn't ask you right, but I'd really like you to come with me to the cook-off. I am a little rough around the edges when it comes to women.''

When she sat, watching him put on his unmatched socks, he shot her a grin of undiluted satisfaction. There was excitement dancing around him like hundred-volt electricity.

Diana sipped her coffee slowly, while Mac drank his quickly. He motioned to the stack of buckwheat pancakes in the center of the table. ''Help yourself— you're too thin.''

That statement rankled. Who was he to criticize her? ''By whose standards?''

''Mine,'' he stated flatly. ''You look like a good wind would blow you up the canyon.''

''You're the wrong sex for a nanny,'' she shot back hotly. ''And I don't need a Dutch uncle, either.''

Suddenly, she panicked. She blinked, horrified at her tumbled emotions. Mac had a knack for knocking her off her isolated perch. Since she'd met him just last night, he'd managed to disrupt her plans for a restful solitary vacation. And he had succeeded in making her explode with anger—and respond to his blatant masculinity.

He leaned back in his chair, eyeing her speculatively. ''Look, if we knew each other well enough, I'd give you that fight you're spoiling for,'' he began reasonably. ''But as it is, it may have to wait until later; then, when I know what's got you so riled, I'll tangle with you. To your heart's content. Whatever makes you happy. But right now, all I can promise you is Benevolence's Fall Hunt Festival. What do you say?''

She eyed him, feeling slightly guilty about snapping at him. Holding grudges did not sit comfortably with her. "I'll think about it."

"You do that," he murmured almost smugly. "I'll pack up my chili while you freshen up. By the way—" he looked at her rumpled jeans and wrinkled sweater "—wear some dancing shoes."

"I haven't agreed to anything, Mac."

He shrugged, grinning down at her. "Neither have I. But folks around here like to think of me as an old widower. Just once I'd like to knock them on their backsides by turning up with a pretty woman like you."

Diana never strayed out of her path for an escapade in her life. For some reason, today she felt like doing just that. Mac might have the wrong approach, but the adventure had a certain lure. . . .

Mac winked with the air of a conspirator. "What do you say, kid?"

She frowned, turning the matter over carefully within her.

A warm finger touched her between her brows and trailed down her nose. She looked up to see Mac's gentle expression. "Frowning causes wrinkles. Haven't you heard? Give it a rest, Diana—for today?"

"Maybe I can't," she answered honestly.

"Maybe you can," he said evenly. "Try."

Diana stared into his dark eyes and decided that maybe she did need a breather, after all. She'd been on a fun-restricted diet, and the opportunity to fudge was enormously appealing. "Count me in," she agreed.

In Mac's four-wheel-drive pickup an hour later, Diana was forced to sit right up against him. She held his Stetson on her lap, protecting it from the musket rifles, which leaned precariously on the passenger door. The notorious bagpipes, on the seat beside her, poked her ribs. She glared up at Mac. "You're taking advantage of the situation."

"Oh, sure. Accuse me of ulterior motives—that's just like a woman." He glanced down at her, then back at the winding highway. "Be reasonable, Diana. I had to put the chili cooker on the floor, and the only place my musket rifles will fit is up against the door like that—by the way, you'll like the black powder shoot—so, the only place left for you to sit was right next to me."

Mac drove leisurely, allowing Diana to view the scenery—tumbling creeks, heavily bordered by white aspens and red pines. Mac tugged her closer.

"See that peak?" he asked, nodding his head toward a rugged mountain. "There are bighorns up there, above the timberline. Deer and elk are coming down from the mountains now, headed for warmer fields. And old Mr. Black Bear is fat from berries, getting ready for his winter nap."

Diana stiffened, pulling her shoulder away from him. Mac seemed to like fitting her to his side, but she wasn't certain just how to handle this much of him at close range. Is this how it begins with men and women? she wondered frantically, trying to place inches between their bodies.

The close confines of the pickup were filled with his scent—wood smoke, soap and tangy after-shave. Mac moved, bringing his side against her. He was like a fresh wind sweeping out the stale air. It had been years since she'd felt feminine . . . and excited.

But she didn't want to feel any of that. She just wanted strength to plot out her life.

"See that creek, Diana? One of the miners back in 1858 first spotted gold nuggets in that creek. Benevolence was named after a gold mine, back in the mining boom. There was a Ute uprising that scared off most of the homesteaders before the turn of the century. Benevolence was a ghost town until the tourist trade discovered us."

Diana shifted again but still felt his hard thigh move when he braked, then accelerated the pickup.

"You're quiet—no one could accuse you of being a magpie. What are you thinking?" he asked.

The honest answer frightened her. She'd been thinking about the way his body moved against her, the way his heat was seeping through her clothes. Instead, Diana ducked her head, feeling suddenly shy. "It's beautiful here, Mac."

"Uh-huh. I grew up here with my brothers, J.D. and Rafe. Rafe's playing at being semi-retired near here. And J.D. is a Denver businessman. Denver may suit J.D., but I wouldn't live anywhere but here." He took a deep breath, a man obviously pleased with his life.

He scanned the fields surrounding the highway. His fingers tightened on her shoulder. "Deer grazing over there. See them?"

"They're so graceful," she said as the deer raised their heads to watch them. "Do you hunt them with those big bows on your wall?"

"Compound bows with more pound power than you must weigh. Yes, I used to hunt. I was a guide and a pretty good tracker. Guess it's the Ute blood in me."

"Where did you learn to play the bagpipes?" she asked, suddenly wanting to know more.

He shrugged. "My grandfather was a Scotsman—the bagpipes were his. The Ute and Spanish blood come from my mother's side. The Spanish explored this country, you know."

He looked down at her, his eyes narrowing. "I'm part hot-blooded Spanish lover. What do you think about that?" he asked suggestively, raising his eyebrows.

His cocky leer caused her to giggle for the first time in years. She felt giddy. "I think you're as windy as your bagpipes, MacLean," she shot back, grinning.

"Whoops! You smiled," he teased, tugging her hair. "I was wondering if you had one locked inside you."

Despite herself, Diana smiled again and looked away.

Catching the scent of his chili, Mac also caught an appealing idea. With Diana on his arm, Ms. Simpson just might take a second taste of his deserving chili. The elderly judge was a romantic right down to her lace pantalets. The first thing he'd do would be to talk to Ray. Ray had badgered him about buying an expensive compound bow he owned; bribing him to play along would be easy.

Immediately upon their arrival at the town hall, Mac installed his electric slow cooker—filled with chili—in the enormous kitchen. Other pots bubbled and steamed, all in a row. Mac lovingly stirred his concoction with a wooden spoon but he took the time out to speak privately with Ray. Then he began introducing Diana to his friends as his "lady." Diana was stunned. "What are you doing, MacLean?" she had asked between her teeth when they were alone.

"Huh?" He glanced at Ms. Simpson, who stared at them over the top of her glasses. He took Diana's hand and kissed the back of it before she could withdraw it.

"Mac! What are you doing?" she repeated, rubbing the lingering warmth of his mouth away.

"Don't look now. See Ms. Simpson over there? The gray-haired lady with the bun? She's the judge of the contest."

Diana tilted her head, feeling as though she had stepped into the Twilight Zone. "What does she have to do with the fact that you just kissed my hand?"

"She's a romantic, Diana," he explained flatly, as though she would instantly understand. "With you next to me, I could win the contest."

Diana stared up at him, taken aback by his tender loverlike smile. She felt a little flutter around her heart. Mac's obvious loneliness had touched her last night. To be Mac's lady for a day wouldn't cost her an ounce of pride. After all, her visit was temporary, and she could manage a little kindness along the way. If he wanted to win the chili contest so badly he'd stay up all night making it, she could manage to play along. *If* he didn't go to extremes.

"Okay, I'll pretend to be your girlfriend," she whispered as he slid his hand to the back of her neck. The possessive gesture caused her skin to tingle. "Just don't overdo it, will you?"

He glanced appraisingly at Ms. Simpson again. "She's a real tough cookie, Diana. Do you think you could help a little?" he asked, pulling her up against him.

Tucked under his arm, his fingers at her waist, Diana had to remind herself that Mac really did need her help. His chili needed her help, she corrected. "I'm here, aren't I?" she asked, trying to wedge space between their bodies.

"Yes, you are. And you just don't know how thankful I am for whatever help you can give me." He scowled at another rancher. "Donaldson, over there, has been walking off with the trophy for years. I'd give a lot to set him on his ear—"

Ray wandered by, smiling widely. "Howdy, Mac. Howdy, Ms. Phillips. Everything okay?"

Mac took a deep breath. "Dandy."

Ray's smile grew. "I'd like my bow as soon as possible, son. Put a ribbon on it, a red one."

"Right. Talk to you later, Ray. Now leave my lady and me alone, okay?"

"Sure, just don't forget our bargain."

Ray moved off into the crowd, and Mac turned to his chili. He glanced at Diana. "You might as well know. I had to bribe him not to tell everyone why you're staying with me."

"Mac..." she began, beginning to question her own sanity. Why on earth had she agreed to this conspiracy?

"I do want that trophy. I've wanted it for years," Mac said softly, slowly. "Now is my one chance."

His tone was just wistful enough to sink her resistance. Diana paused in midbreath and changed her refusal to a simple, "I know. You owe me, though. Just how are you going to explain my getaway?"

"Simple. We'll have a doozy of a fight. You get mad and leave." Mac saw Ms. Simpson easing her way to them through the crowd. "Could we, ah, talk about this later? I really need to talk to Ms. Simpson. Something about a secret spice."

When he returned a few minutes later, Diana found him watching her intently. He had a thoughtful expression that totally unsettled her. "Exactly why are you looking at me like that, Mac?" she asked carefully.

He took her plate from her and placed it on the bench beside him. Taking both her hands, he held them between his own. "Diana, I made sure Ms. Simpson knew that you were my girlfriend."

Mac had the same look her boys did just before they admitted their guilt about something. "And?"

He shook his head. "It didn't seem to affect her. Being my girlfriend isn't enough. I have to come up with something else fast to turn the contest my way."

Diana took a deep breath, trying to withdraw her hands. She didn't like her sinking premonition. Not a bit. "And?"

His fingers tightened as he frowned. "We need to show her we're really serious about each other. We need to be believable. Do you think you could manage a great big kiss?"

"A kiss? Mac!"

"Shh! Don't get excited. It's just the edge I need—"

"You need a straitjacket."

"Haven't you ever wanted anything bad?" he asked urgently, scanning the crowd.

She shook her head. "Let go of my hands so I can—"

A cluster of giggling teenagers passed, keeping Diana from telling Mac just what he could kiss. "You're single-minded, Mac," she finally said. "You can take your contest and—"

Ray walked up to them, munching on a carrot stick. "Problems, Mac?"

Mac glared at the clerk. "Not a one. Everything is smooth as good bourbon. Go away."

While Diana was still trying to plan her escape, Mac turned back to her and whispered, "We really need one big kiss to put this whole thing over."

"You're not getting one, Mac. You just back off," Diana firmly asserted just before the black powder shoot-out was announced.

Mac stared at her, lifting one eyebrow. "You're not afraid, are you?" he asked mildly. "I didn't think you could last out the day."

His challenge hit Diana broadside. Feeling a full tide of fury wash over her, she announced too quietly, "I can take anything you can dish out, cowboy."

"Huh," he said simply as he led her outside to the target range. "A good kiss would—"

"Oh, shut up," Diana ordered curtly. She wondered how she could steal his pickup and drive back to the ranch, get her bags and drive away in her car.

Everyone in Benevolence seemed to have a match-making twinkle in his eyes, Diana noticed. It seemed that the woman occupying Mac MacLean's strong arm was more of a curiosity than a two-headed calf. She felt as though she were being mobbed, with a smiling Ms. Simpson leading the crowd.

On the target range, Mac held out a seven-foot musket to her, his eyes daring her. Because she was angry, Diana jerked it from his hands, then struggled to aim the heavy barrel at the target. Mac's arms moved around her to support the musket.

The intimate position implied a blazing love affair, firing Diana's temper. She pulled the trigger impatiently; the blast knocked her back into his waiting arms.

Mac cursed. Then his hands trembling, he embraced her tightly. "Damn, I should have known. Are you hurt, Diana?" he demanded fiercely, pressing his lean cheek against her soft one.

Diana pulled away from him, feeling the sensual warmth begin to flow through her. "Let me go, Mac," she said huskily, wondering if her legs could carry her to the nearby benches. The tantalizing ripples sweeping inside her intensified.

Through taut lips, he whispered, "Now, Diana. Don't go making mountains out of molehills. You're getting all worked up when all I want is a kiss."

"You deliberately maneuvered me into this." A flush traveled from her face downward. Her nipples hardened in response to his staring at her mouth.

"Since you're mad anyway..." He gathered her into his arms as if he had the right to have her locked against him. He ignored the thrust of her palms against his stomach, and his lips touched hers tenderly.

For a moment, she stared into his eyes, felt the warmth of his face on hers, the gentle hand supporting her head. Diana's anger wavered, then vanished as his mouth began to move over hers. Her lids closed and her senses ached with unfulfilled hunger. It plagued her, causing her finger to coil around his belt. She forgot everything but his searing touch.

His hand slid down her back, urging her nearer.

She thought she heard a sigh and recognized it as her own. When Mac reluctantly ended the kiss, he gazed at her with undisguised need. His eyes darkened as a dull flush rose in his lean cheeks. "I didn't mean for that to happen. At least not that way, Diana," he admitted slowly.

Diana's knees threatened to buckle; her breath was coming unevenly. She forced a swallow and moistened her dry lips. Never in her entire life had any man looked as longingly at her as Mac did just then. He was like a starving man viewing a banquet.

The musket shots rang out, and the pungent scent of sulfur floated by on the cold mountain air. Mac's gaze wandered down her slight body appraisingly, and she found she could no more stop her eyes from blazing the same trail down his body than she could stop the winter snows. Diana felt the world slip away; everything around them was blocked out by Mac's broad shoulders looming nearer.

Carefully, Mac drew her to him once more. Through the layers of their clothing, she felt his tense anticipation. "Now you've done it," he murmured huskily, lowering his mouth to hers.

Something new and utterly delicious quivered within her as he tasted her delicately. When his hand slid beneath her denim jacket to caress her back, she moved deeper into his arms.

His breath was warm, fanning her cheek. The kiss went gently on, destroying her defenses, taking away the pain . . . and replacing it with hunger.

His taut body was trembling when he released her reluctantly. His sultry gaze traveled over her upturned face, lingering on her swollen lips.

When the cheer went up, the two looked around and saw they were surrounded by spectators.

"Just what you wanted." Diana was frightened suddenly and unable to move back from his light embrace. New emotions hit her like a blast of hot dry desert wind. She'd forgotten the power of a man's sensuality, the needs stirring within her. She'd kept them wrapped up for too long, and now this Colorado cowboy had reached right into the tender bruised heart of her.

"I didn't intend it to turn out that way," he said cautiously.

Mac drew her behind a weathered aspen tree. His forefinger lightly trailed down her cheek, tracing the fullness of her bottom lip. "What's wrong? Was it so awful?" he murmured intimately.

She shivered when he caressed her nape. Mac seemed to know where to touch her. "You're shaking," he whispered gently.

"We're standing in front of a lot of people, Mac. Making out in front of a crowd," she said unevenly, glancing away. "Like teenagers."

He smiled. "Be glad they're here. It's the best protection you could have."

Unable to meet his tender stare, Diana watched the crowd move toward the town hall. "They're leaving, Mac."

"Uh-huh. It's judging time for the cook-off."

"Aren't you entering your chili, Mac?"

His eyes widened in surprise. "Shoot. I'd forgotten. Come on."

Mac insisted Diana stay near him as Ms. Simpson tasted the enormous selection of chili. The contest was finally narrowed to Donaldson and Mac.

Donaldson, a big man with a round stomach, elbowed Mac. "I've got it sewed up this year, Mac. Had some green chilies imported from Texas and added my special spice." He grinned. "It's called edge, son. Of course, I'm not sporting that little piece on my arm."

Mac glared at him. "Cut it, Donaldson. Diana and I are getting married. And I imported some Idaho sweet onions the size of footballs especially for this—"

"Married?" The rancher and Diana interrupted jointly.

"Why, sure." Mac drew Diana closer to his side. "Did everybody hear that?" he called out to everybody. "Diana and I have just gotten engaged. We're getting married. We'll put together a shindig this town has never seen for a wedding."

A cheer went from up the crowd.

"Mac, can we talk?" Diana said weakly.

"Later, honey. They're judging the cook-off right now. And I want to be here to get *my* trophy."

"Oh, that's the edge, Mac. Not the onions," Donaldson growled. The two tall men pressed Diana between them as they glared at each other. "You know you'll get old Ms. Simpson's vote once she finds out you're finally getting hitched. She's a sucker for romance. And she's been trying for years to find somebody who would have your cantankerous self. Who could resist a hermit in love?" he scoffed. "Of all the low, conniving—"

The angry rancher's cheeks puffed out, his short beard standing out like porcupine quills. "This is worse than the time you sabotaged my chili with that bottle of cheap hot sauce and added vinegar to boot," Donaldson accused.

"It was so weak, it needed something for body," Mac returned. "What about the time you dumped a bag of chili mix—"

"Married?" Diana repeated, feeling as if she'd been dropped into never-never land.

Mac glanced down at her as though he'd just remembered something—her. "That's right, honey. We are engaged, you know. As soon as we can, we'll go up to Creede and get a ring."

Diana felt numb. A full-fledged Colorado wild man wanted to marry her. A rancher who played bagpipes on Halloween and stayed up brewing his chili all night. She stared up at Mac's clean-shaved jaw. Hard-nosed determination lodged in every bone in his tall lean body. *Mac wanted that trophy.*

Donaldson threw another verbal jab. "That time you rappelled down the face of that canyon wall, Mac, I should have cut the rope."

"I was after your ewe, Donaldson. That bighorn sheep would have splattered her all over the face of that rock," Mac growled back. "What about those poachers hunting on your spread last year? I helped locate them, didn't I?"

"'Help'? Is that what you call it? Boy, your copter scared my Herefords into a stampede. Ran fifty pounds of good fat off of each one. I could have handled those lamebrain trophy hunters by myself." Donaldson's massive jowls shook as Ms. Simpson tasted Mac's chili and slowly smiled.

When Ms. Simpson took another delicate spoonful, Donaldson's three-hundred-pound frame seemed to vibrate. "You play those damned bagpipes this year, and I won't donate a cent to the city's old-time boardwalk."

"Mac?" Diana called softly.

Mac snorted, slipping his big hand around Diana's numb fingers. "Huh. Big deal. I already donated the money."

When Ms. Simpson sampled Donaldson's chili, Mac stopped growling and raised Diana's fingers to his mouth. He frowned, rubbing his lips across the smooth back of her hand. "What's wrong, honey? Your fingers are like ice. Aren't you warm enough?" He touched her forehead with his palm. "No fever. Diana, what's wrong?"

Diana felt the real world spinning away from her. "Married?" she finally managed to say just as Ms. Simpson raised the trophy.

A guilty expression crossed Mac's face. His black eyes shifted away from Diana's accusing ones. "I was stuck," he whispered. "The marriage was a stroke of genius—Donaldson was right, I needed an edge to win. He's got some secret spice grown by his Mexican housekeeper. All I had was you,'' he said desperately. ''You've got to help me.''

For a moment Diana wondered if she could reach high enough to dump Mac's chili over his head. ''You—''

''That's it! That's good, Diana. Let all those hostilities come out,'' he said, looking around anxiously. ''But not here.''

Ms. Simpson's voice crackled over the microphone. ''We have this year's winner—Mac MacLean!''

Donaldson cursed and the crowd cheered.

Locking his fingers with Diana's, Mac dragged her to the waiting judges. Scooping her against him and lifting her feet from the wooden floor, Mac raised his trophy in his free hand. He kissed her on the cheek, then grinned boyishly at the crowd. ''Thanks to my good luck charm, my future wife, Diana.''

He kissed her full on the lips, then whispered softly, ''Don't worry about anything, Diana. I've got everything under control.''

Three

It's about time, Mac," Ms. Simpson cooed. She turned to Diana. "Congratulations, young lady, I didn't think Mac would ever get around to proposing to another woman. We've all been afraid that he'd live alone forever, waste away up there on that ranch."

The old woman peered up at Mac, who was accepting hearty congratulations from his friends. She confided to Diana, "He's a nice boy. Took care of his ailing parents and tended his wife until the day she died. Poor Eleanor, she just wasn't suited to that rough ranch life. I couldn't be happier for you both. Now, if we could just marry those other brothers, Rafe and J.D. Heartbreakers, all three of them. When the MacLean boys were about, you could always count on some poor girl losing her heart."

Smiling with a happiness she did not feel, Diana managed to reply, "Mac hasn't exactly asked—"

Donaldson gave her a bear hug, almost lifting her off her feet. He grinned at Mac's outraged expression. "The poor thing looks confused, Mac. Of course, after smelling your chili all night, she probably needs detoxification. Maybe she'll keep you from running that damned copter all across the county at all hours of the night. Good luck, boy."

Once freed from Donaldson, Diana fought for breath as she secretly checked her ribs. She looked up at Mac, keeping her lips pasted in a smile. "I'd like to talk to you privately, please, Mac."

His thick eyebrows went up, showing his surprise. "But, Diana, they just asked me to play the bagpipes to start the dancing."

Diana controlled her rising need to scream. The muscles of her face hurt with tension as she valiantly maintained the smile. "I feel like blowing up, Mac," she enunciated slowly. "And I may. Right here in front of your chili-eating friends. You could lose the trophy by default."

Mac stooped a little to examine her closely. He frowned. "Is something wrong, Diana?"

She nodded, still smiling.

"Uh-huh. Well, they're all waiting for the dancing to begin."

Through her teeth, Diana asked, "Could they possibly begin without you, Mac?"

He rubbed his jaw, studying her. "I don't know. The Hunter's Bash has never opened without me before. Not since I got back from Nam."

Donaldson's beefy shoulder nudged Mac's arm. "We'll struggle along without you this year, Mac. Go on, the little lady obviously has something to say. Maybe she'd like to skip the bagpipes, too."

Mac found an empty office, and he and Diana went inside. He closed the door behind them. Standing in a corner, Diana wrapped her arms around her chest and glared up at him. "Just where do you get off, big man?" she asked tightly.

Mac slipped his hands in his back pockets, then leaned against a wall. "You're upset."

"That's an understatement." Diana felt her temper begin to flare. The "house mouse," as Alex had named her, was turning into a lion. "I'm on vacation, Mac. I didn't come to make a fool of an entire town."

He shrugged, his expression wary. "I know that."

She tapped the toe of one small jogger. "Tell me what else you know. Just so I won't waste time repeating the facts to you."

"I know that you're scared, Diana, on the run from yourself. . . . I know that I want to help."

Stunned by his admission, Diana shook her head, trying to clear it. She fought confusion. She looked at Mac's face, his high cheekbones, that sensuous mouth and hard jaw. "You don't know me, Mac, and I don't know a thing about you," she said, unable to glance away from him. "I'm not shopping for good Samaritans."

"I know everything I need to know about you, Diana Phillips. I lost a lot of buddies in Nam, and I learned that you'd better grab friendships when you can."

She cleared her dry throat, wondering if she was dreaming. Who was crazy here? Had she missed something? "Lying to everyone inside this town hall is not the way to keep friendships. And I know what being lied to is like."

"Maybe I did put my foot in it." Mac took a step toward her, keeping his hands in his jeans pockets. His eyes blazed down at her. "Blame it on my wanting to win the chili trophy. I'm high on a well-deserved victory."

"You're playing games, while I'm . . ." She struggled for the right words to make him understand. "Mac, I'm trying to stand on my own feet. I'm trying to fit all the pieces together. I need peace."

Floundering in a jumble of emotions, Diana flung out her hand, and somehow it grazed his flat stomach. She jerked her fingers away, as though they had been burned.

The heat of his body reached out to her as Mac took another step nearer. She tilted her head back. "Mac," she began to protest as his head lowered. "I'm not up to this. Games aren't for me."

"I wouldn't hurt you for the world." Mac's lips touched hers lightly in a brief kiss.

When he straightened, Diana forced herself to gaze at the first button of his shirt. She wanted to place her arms around him and snuggle against his broad chest. She swallowed the lump of need drying her throat.

"Your husband really did a job on you, didn't he?"

Diana began to shake, desperately fighting to keep her distance. She was raw and bleeding, and knowing instinctively that Mac could soothe her made it that much harder to stay away.

"Diana Phillips, stay with me for a time. Let me be your friend?" Mac asked gently. "Why don't you wrap your arms around me and hold on tight."

She shook her head, and Mac sighed deeply. "My hands are in my pockets. Come on, trust me enough to tell me about it."

Diana looked up at him. She had to keep all her secrets locked inside. Just until she had turned them around, studied them and put them in order. "Not now, Mac."

"I'll be here when you want to talk. That's what friends are for." Mac's lips lifted in a wry smile.

Suddenly, Diana felt young and shy and uncertain. Her lashes fluttered, and she felt her hands move.

Beside her ear, Mac whispered, "Put them on my face. Touch me. You've been looking at my mouth for a time now, so kiss me, too. If you like."

When she looked up at him warily, Mac added, "So far as I know, no one ever died from a kiss. In fact, it was a kiss that awoke Sleeping Beauty."

Diana couldn't resist sneaking a look at Mac's firm lips. She'd walked in the cold loneliness for an eternity. Now the gentleness in Mac's face offered her solace.

Taking a step, Diana placed her body against him lightly. She eased her cheek to that safe, warm chest and heard the rapid beating of his heart.

"That's it," he murmured, his jaw nuzzling the top of her head. "Rest awhile."

Diana slid her arms around his waist. For just this moment, Mac was her harbor in the storm.

His arms closed around her slowly, lightly. Broad palms stroked her back and shoulders, soothing her as he rocked her in his arms.

Then the tears came, the ones she'd fought for so long. They trailed down her cheeks and fell on his skin. She rubbed his chest with her cheek, trying to dry the tears. "I'm sorry."

She heard a rough sound and felt Mac's chest lifting and falling unevenly beneath her head. "Oh, honey," he said, the husky timbre telling her he understood her pain and loneliness, as though her aching heart were his own. She looked up through her veil of tears, her fingers seeking his face. Mac stood absolutely still as she touched his damp cheeks.

"Why?" she asked, then remembered how he'd lost his wife.

He tilted his head and kissed her fingers. "I'm a softy," he whispered raggedly. "Lord, honey, there's enough pain in you to last a lifetime."

"I'm afraid," she returned, tracing his lips, entranced by the hard yet sensitive line.

Mac cradled her cheek in the palm of his hand. She felt the rough skin and calluses. "Please don't be afraid."

Her mouth met his, and she felt his breath on her cheek. This time, Mac's lips moved firmly across hers. Leaning back in his arms, Diana savored his kisses, waited for the sweet calming glow...

Her hands swept slowly across his back, and she felt the hard muscles ripple beneath her touch. Mac shuddered, pulling her hips nearer his thighs, fitting her into his long body.

Diana's breath caught when her breasts pressed against his chest. Then Mac groaned, a ragged masculine sound that spoke of his need. His lips parted and his tongue darted hungrily into her mouth, as though he needed her essence.

Diana moved against his hard form. Mac cradled her, sliding one big hand low on her back.

Incredible heat began to throb inside her, burning through the clothes separating them. She groaned, aching, and he murmured something roughly, his fingers sliding between them.

Gently, his hand cupped her breast. Mac sighed and trailed tiny kisses from the corners of her lips to her ear. He was breathing heavily as his fingers moved across the delicate slopes of her breasts.

Trembling with the effort, Diana pulled back and gazed up at his face. "No," she said simply, and Mac responded with a nod. She touched his hair, felt the silky strands glide through her fingers as she eased them back from his temple.

Mac's hand slid to her cheek. "You're shaking. This is all new to me, too." She blushed and tucked her head beneath his chin.

"Don't worry," he murmured gently. "We'll work everything out."

He gave her a playful smacking kiss that made her tingle all over. "Friends?"

Friends. Not once in her lifetime had a man asked friendship of her. Possession was the main rule in her relationship with Alex. What were Mac's rules?

"Back to this marriage thing," he was saying. "It has a certain appeal to a man in my condition."

Diana jumped out of his arms like a scalded cat. "But it's out of the question. We don't know each other." Diana felt her knees begin to weaken as his darkened gaze traveled down her body, resting on her breasts.

"You're afraid to stay the week you'd planned."

"You are hardheaded, Mac," she said, wondering vaguely how this one man could stir her passions so quickly.

"A week-long engagement with a wham-bang fight at the end. We can fight over squeezing the toothpaste tube at the wrong end, or something. You can fly off free as a bird. If you still want to, then."

Diana closed her eyes, suddenly weary to her bones. She leaned against the wall for support.

Mac took her hand and led her to the couch. "Rest awhile with me. Let me take care of you."

She searched his gentle expression and found only concern. "Mac, this is unreal. It must be the elevation."

"Nope. The only thing that's unreal is your past." He winked with the air of a conspirator. "What do you say? Want to go along with my plan, or do you want to spoil my big day? Just a week?"

How could this stranger know her so well? she wondered. "Does Donaldson really have a secret spice?"

"Hell, yes! I've tried to find out what it is for years. But now I've got you," he announced cheerfully. "Are you game?"

"You've already got the trophy. Why—"

"I'd just like to set this town on its collective ear, that's all. They've been calling me a hermit for years." A shadow crossed his face. "Ever since my wife died."

In an abrupt change of mood, he grinned widely, placing his hand over his chest dramatically. "I'll be heartbroken when you leave in a snit. Of course, every single woman in the valley will probably come calling with fresh-baked pies."

Diana giggled, drawn by his comic appeal. "You are a con man, Mac."

Staring at her intently, Mac whispered huskily, "I could use a friend, too, Diana. How about it?"

Their eyes met and held. "Maybe," she agreed softly. "For a week."

The band began playing, and music floated into the office. Diana leaned on Mac's shoulder, content for a moment. "They started without your bagpipes."

He kissed her forehead. "So they did. I'll play the songs for you later at the house."

She smiled softly, wondering if Mac could really be her friend. "I can't wait."

He grinned. "Ready to get back in there and dance? I'm pretty rusty, but I'll try."

"I haven't danced in years, Mac. I'm not sure I know how."

"Trust me. You'll remember."

Diana ran her palm along his cheek. *Her friend?* "You ask a lot, Mac."

At one o'clock in the morning, Mac turned the pickup into his driveway, the frozen landscape no longer seeming lonely to him. Diana's head rested against his shoulder, her breath tickling the hair at the

base of his neck. She had snuggled to him so easily—
he liked that.

He'd studied her all night, watching her dance and
laugh. When she thought he wasn't looking, Diana
had sneaked wary curious glances at him.

She'd been on a nervous high for hours, and the instant they began to drive home, her head settled
peacefully onto his shoulder and she quickly fell
asleep.

His mouth turned down. Mac's gut instinct had told
him to make the announcement, using it to snare the
chili trophy. He'd almost scared her to death, he
should have known better.

He liked her soft mouth moving beneath his. . . .

Mac eased Diana's sleeping body into his arms and
carried her into the house.

Wanting attention, Red whined and nuzzled Mac's
legs as Mac placed Diana on the bed. He looked at her
pale face on the pillow. She belonged here, he decided, tugging off her shoes and socks.

He eased off her jacket and slid her under the blankets. Diana slept heavily throughout.

Mac had to force himself to leave her. He stoked the
woodstove in the kitchen, making it warmer than
usual for her. Then he sat looking out the windows as
he rubbed Red's shaggy head. "It wouldn't be too
bad, old dog. Having her around for a while."

Diana coming into his arms was one of the sweetest
things to happen in his life. . . .

Mac settled deeper in his chair, remembering his
anger at the man who had hurt Diana. Shaking his
head, he looked down at Red. "I intend to keep her

for a time. After all, it does a man good to shake people up once in a while."

Finally, when he could resist no longer, Mac went into the bedroom to watch his lady sleep. Red whined and followed.

Mac watched Diana in the dim light coming from the hallway. Her face turned toward him. She sighed, stirring restlessly. Would she wake in the night and leave him? Panic rippled inside him. His heart seemed to stop beating. He had to keep her, somehow.

Without a second thought, Mac eased himself on the bed on top of the blankets and drew the quilt over him. Taking care in the small space, he laid an arm and a leg over Diana. There, he thought, now she wouldn't be able to get away without waking him. He closed his eyes, praying she would choose to stay.

Her hair clung to his cheek, its scent fresh and feminine. He savored the softness within his arms, realizing the depth of his own loneliness. In the dreamy realm between reality and sleep, he wondered how it would feel to hold her every night.

He dozed, but when she stirred, Mac jumped out of bed, feeling a jolt of pure panic race through him. Would she stay? There wasn't a thing he could do if she decided to leave.

Diana's brown eyes opened slowly. She stared at him blankly for a moment. "Hi, Mac," she murmured drowsily. "You're here again."

He adjusted the covers around her, his hands trembling. "I hope you're not cold. You shouldn't be. You've got two blankets wrapped around you."

She lifted her arms, stretching and yawning. The vulnerable line of her throat caused Mac's mouth to dry. Diana in the morning was very sensuous. To wake up to her every morning would be an adventure in itself.

"Why are you so nice, Mac?" she asked.

"Because you're mine to take care of. I found you on my front porch. It's that simple," he answered honestly. "Do you want to talk now?"

She stared at him for a long moment, with sleepy eyes. "About what?"

He shivered. "I'm cold. Do you think you can spare a little warmth for a freezing man?"

She looked away from him, her black lashes sheltering her expression. "I'm not up to any of that, you know."

He took her chin in his hand. "I haven't asked a thing but a blanket on a cold November morning. That, and helping me put one over on Benevolence."

Diana sat up and stared out of the window, her expression that of pain. "There have been too many people asking too many things of me, Mac," she whispered slowly. "Who am I, really? I don't know anymore."

The aching tone cut at Mac, and he wanted to hold her. Instead, taking care not to alarm her, he sat down on a chair. "We'll find out, honey. But I can tell you this—you've got an independent streak in you a mile wide."

"Not now. It's gone—I'm too tired." They were both quiet for a while. Then she smiled at him and handed him the quilt, which he wrapped around him. "You know, I haven't slept with my clothes on since I was a little girl."

He chuckled. "It's been some time since I lay in bed with all my clothes on, too. I think it was when I was about ten and had sneaked out for some moonlight dogsledding with Red's grandfather. My brothers and I had to be up early for chores, and we didn't want the folks to know, so we slept in our clothes. That was one long day."

He talked easily, knowing that the sound of his voice soothed her. That was all that mattered as daylight slipped into the bedroom. "Old Red's grandfather was a purebred McKenzie River husky. His grandmother was a Coppermine husky, and both of them knew how to pull better than any dog team around. There's an old Yukon-type sled in the barn—about seven feet long. As boys, my brothers and I used to hitch up the dogs and let them run. We had five dogs then, all in working weight in the winter. That was for rescue on the mountains, before snowmobiles."

Diana shifted and sighed. Mac's heart skipped a beat when he realized that if the engagement was real, he could hold her every day, every night. It was a thought that slid over him like dark sweet honey; it lingered and tantalized. He had to fight to keep from taking her in his arms. "Boring, huh?"

"No," she answered sleepily. She sighed again, her lashes drifting down. "Please, Mac, continue."

The scent of her hair was exotic and irresistible. Mac wanted to slide his fingers through it, taste the silky skin of her neck. Instead, he forced himself to talk. "Each dog can pull about two hundred pounds. There's a small birch sleigh in the barn, too. When you want, honey, we'll harness Red and take you out for a run. There's nothing like it—the sun hitting the snow, the cold freezing on your face. It's like catching a dream. You forget everything but the sleigh gliding over the snow, the dogs running, pulling the sled.''

Diana dozed and Mac felt sleep overcoming him, too. Yawning, he wrapped the warmth of her nearness around him and drifted off into the first peaceful sleep he'd had in years.

Mac awoke in a panic, feeling the empty bed. He scrambled to his feet and raced to the front door, his heart slamming against his chest. Red barked excitedly, leaping around his legs as Mac jerked open the door and ran out onto the porch. ''Damn! She's gone, isn't she?'' Mac scanned the road, looking for Diana and knowing she'd left him.

He felt a movement behind him and pivoted, almost closing the door on Diana's surprised face. He stepped back into the house. ''Where have you been?'' he demanded roughly, placing his hands on his hips.

Her dark delicate eyebrows lifted; her expression was indignant. ''Who wants to know?'' she shot back. ''It would serve you right if I drove out today and made you the laughing stock of Benevolence. How would you explain that one, big guy?''

Because she'd scared him so badly, Mac felt raw. He frowned, breathing heavily. ''You weren't this mad last night. Why are you now?''

She looked him up and down, her gaze meeting his evenly. ''Why am I mad, he asks? You knew I was tired, and you wore me down with your talk of concern. Like a brainwasher, or something. But that was yesterday. Now I've had some rest, and I'm furious.

You used me. You took advantage of me. If you ever—repeat, ever—put me in a position like you did yesterday, I just don't know what I'll do. But it won't be pleasant!''

Something within him sang. He liked the cocky tilt of her head, the flashing dark brown eyes and temper staining her cheeks. She was so alive, every ounce of her held fire. "Now, Diana," he began, taking a step toward her.

Diana jabbed his chest with her finger, tilting her head back to glare at him. "You snore," she accused firmly. "Big dragging snores. Like a walrus on land. I had to move to the couch."

Mac blinked. For a moment she had him off balance. In his lifetime, few women had come at him like a cornered bobcat. "Are we in a snit?" he asked carefully, examining the sleek lines of her legs beneath her cotton-knit skirt.

"That's putting it delicately. You're sneaky—you creep up on people when they're bone tired."

"Maybe you're right," he returned. Watching Diana lay down the law with the morning sun outlining her slender legs was sheer pleasure. "Wait until I have my morning coffee, and I'll argue with you about anything you want."

"I'm not comfortable about this week-long farce at all. Even though I can walk out at any time and leave you to play the fool. My honor is at stake." She breathed heavily, pushing back her overlong sleeves impatiently. She stalked around him, gauging him from head to toe. Mac held perfectly still, knowing that Diana needed to turn over everything in her mind.

When she had come full circle, Diana said, "Okay, you want to be friends—I can understand that coming from a hermit. Maybe no one but a stranger would have you for a friend. *You* need me. But I want to know more about you. There's more to life than playing jokes on whole towns, you know. Do you have a job, Mac?"

"Not right now. Unless you count running this ranch."

Her small hand slashed the air impatiently. "Fine. So what is the drawing board and all the whachamacallits doing beneath that sheet in the living room? And the computer?"

Mac took a deep breath and answered her question. "I'm an engineer."

She frowned, digesting his answer. "Why aren't you working in an office? Surely you can't have many clients out here."

"A consulting free-lance engineer. There's a helicopter out back. It's just a hop and a skip to the airport. Some people enjoy concrete mazes and asphalt— I don't."

Diana's dark eyes lighted up. "A helicopter?"

"I flew one in Nam. I have a license."

"You must be good. You probably transmit data with a telephone modem, don't you?"

"Straight from my computer to theirs," he agreed quietly.

"One of the capable ones—a man who can do anything. A chili-cooking, bagpipe-playing, helicopter-flying rancher/engineer. You know just who you are and what you can do, don't you? Just what I need."

She began backing toward the kitchen, her face taut with anger.

He took a step, wanting to hold her. "Now, Diana, don't get all worked up."

She threw up her hands, and he noticed flour dusting her wrists. "'Worked up'? Why would I do that? You had the advantage all the time, didn't you? You know what you want and how to get it. I just walked into your neat little plans to make fools of a whole town. You wanted to use me—I never had a chance."

"I've never taken advantage of a woman in my life, Diana," he stated, feeling the tension in his body. Would she run now? Helpless before her rising temper, Mac decided to keep quiet. He scratched his newly grown beard, contemplating the spitfire before him.

"I'm baking bread. I always bake bread when I'm angry," she said ominously. "Stay out of my way."

"Smells good..." he began gently, then stopped when he saw Diana's hips sway as she walked away from him.

He thrust his hands into his pockets, wanting to cup that gentle softness. Damn, he cursed. She needed to bring out all that long-suppressed anger, and he needed—what? To play her big brother, her friend, her lover? Mac closed his eyes, remembering the feel of her breasts against him.

Then he settled himself on the couch and watched Diana warily over the top of his newspaper. She worked feverishly.

Coming out of the kitchen, Diana studied him. Then she marched straight into the living room and stood squarely in front of him. "I don't owe you a thing but bed and board, mister. You need me, got that? You're lonesome and you've gotten us both into a corner. And I'm the only one who can get you out. Ha!''

She thrust a mug of coffee at him. "I want every last sock you own on the kitchen table in five minutes. My fiancé isn't going to go anywhere wearing those." She pointed to his feet.

Mac wriggled his toes and stared at his socks. "What's wrong with them?"

Diana took a deep breath, exhaling slowly. Mac forced his eyes away from her breasts, which were thrusting at the thin cloth of her shirt. "Other than the left stocking is navy blue and the right one is black with red stripes, nothing is wrong with your socks."

"Are you staying, then, Diana?" he asked quietly, waiting.

"A week. I need to show myself—and you—that I can handle the situation." She looked shyly away from him, the color slowly creeping up her cheeks. He could see her heartbeat pulsing in the hollow in her throat, and he knew that she was thinking of their kisses. How long had it been since she'd been kissed so hungrily? How long had it been since she'd felt wanted as a woman? Somehow he felt it was years.

Meeting his gaze, she added firmly, "Besides, I liked those nice people at the cook-off. They may need protecting from you."

"It will be my pleasure to extend the hospitality of my kingdom to you, ma'am. For as long as it's needed," he answered truthfully and felt the emptiness begin to slide away.

Four

———

Diana breathed the crisp morning air as she picked her way through the blue spruce and aspen trees in the small canyon. In the two days since Mac's announcement of their engagement, she'd taken several long walks with Red. The quiet solitude was restful, and she found her pain easing.

Pulling her jacket collar higher against the cold wind, she thought of her marriage and family. The white picket fence and the all-American dream. She'd given herself to that dream, heart and soul, and now it was gone. She'd pasted her life together, survived by sheer willpower, but now there were odd pieces missing from her life. Somehow, she had to find the strength to make herself whole again.

She stared at the ranch and spotted Mac instantly. "I knew Mac would be outside, Red. Trying to look as though he's checking on the cows, when he's really watching us from beneath that Stetson of his. Spying on us, that's what he does. He acts like a rumpled old badger when we don't invite him on our walks,'' she noted to the husky, who walked close to her heels.

Diana scowled as she approached the barn's feed-lot. The small herd of Herefords looked up at her while Mac turned his back. "See that, Red? Oh, now he's trying to play the innocent."

There was something about Mac that caused her to want to confront him. She liked catching Mac off guard; he got such a sheepish boyish look on his face. "I wouldn't steal your dog, Mac. He's probably your only friend."

Beneath the brim of the Stetson, his heavy brows lifted. He was the picture of innocence. "Who said you would?"

The buffalo bull lumbered toward her and nudged her knee. When she stepped back, frightened by the shaggy mountain of animal, Mac looked up. "That's Old Bob. He's harmless."

"Why on earth—"

Mac shrugged, rubbing the buffalo's large hump roughly. The bull swayed and almost seemed to purr with delight. "I couldn't stand to see him made into buffalo burgers, so I bought him from Donaldson. Pet him—Old Bob likes that."

Tentatively, she stroked the buffalo's head. Mac nodded approvingly, then easily lifted a fifty-pound sack of grain to pour into a feed trough. He looked as though he wanted to say something, but just some-how couldn't.

"Do you have a problem, Mac?" Diana asked quietly, knowing that Mac would answer truthfully. He didn't have a dram of deceit in his large well-muscled body, and Diana had repeatedly tested her new skill of attacking problems face-to-face on him.

"Okay, you asked for it," he said slowly. "You just don't realize what could happen on those precious walks of yours. I know you're working out some pretty serious burrs in your life and need to be alone, but if you fell down a rocky slope or if a wounded bear decided to have you for his supper—"

"Red is always with me, Mac."

"Huh! And what about that jacket?" He reached out and tugged at the denim. "It doesn't even have a flannel lining."

Mac playing mother hen was a sight that warmed Diana's bruised heart. In the few days since she'd arrived, she'd noted his excellent care of the livestock and assorted strays that seemed to head unerringly for his ranch.

But she couldn't allow him to rule her life. Mac sometimes made her feel like a child. But then there were other times when he made her feel... Diana shivered. She felt restless and torn apart. She looked at a tree, comparing the stark leafless limbs to her life.

"You're working at it, aren't you?" he asked softly, running a warm fingertip along her jaw. "Getting all stewed up, working at what's eating you."

"Maybe I am," she answered, stepping away from his disturbing touch.

"Why don't you do something just for the sheer hell of it?" he asked lightly, his eyes glittering.

She laughed, knowing it to be a nervous reaction. "You mean staying with you and playing a game with the innocent people of Benevolence isn't enough?"

"Hell, no," he began. He reached out and ruffled her short hair playfully. "What do you say about running into town and stirring things up?"

Diana smiled. "You realize that after this week, you're going to have a lot of explaining to do?"

When he simply looked at her, she added, "Mac, I'm not a dropout with a million dollars in my pocket. I need to begin looking for work here or somewhere else. Maybe in Denver—"

"My future wife?" Mac felt a cold wave of panic. He couldn't let her out of his grasp now. She'd dropped into his dreary life like a bright tropical flower. "Now, look, Diana. I can provide—"

Diana raised one slender but firm finger. "Don't hallucinate, Mr. MacLean."

"Hell, I'm thinking about our game plan—for appearance's sake," he snapped, knowing she'd reached inside him to touch a live nerve. He'd spent part of the previous night holding her, absorbing the warmth of her body. Now he could feel Diana sliding away. Desperately, he thought of future nights.... "You can't look for work within days of arriving—"

"So you have it, too?" she asked quietly, frowning. "The macho-big guy syndrome—keep the little wife at home and under your thumb. Is that what happened to Eleanor?"

Because Diana was hurting, Mac let the accusation slide off. His marriage with Eleanor had been pure gold. But now she was gone. The horror of her dying had stunned him, and he had slipped into a mechanical life without her.

Then a half-pint stray had come drifting into his empty world and swept the loneliness out of his heart.

He wanted Diana in his home, in his life and in his bed permanently, Mac realized sharply. She'd come to him a stray, but that had all changed. Holding a woman in his arms all night gave a man certain rights, he decided firmly. Kissing the sweetness on her lips and feeling like starting all over again really gave a man ideas about living.

Especially when he started worrying about her leaving. Especially since he'd begun to think of waking up to her every morning like a real husband.

He closed his eyes a moment, allowing the tantalizing fantasy to enfold him. Marriage to Diana would be a spicy delight, a daily confection—

Diana jabbed Mac's flannel-covered chest with her finger. Her mouth pursed but before she could speak, he grabbed her wrist, trapping it securely but gently against his warm body. "Is that what happened to you?" he said.

Diana stepped back from him, her back meeting the weathered boards of the old barn. She stiffened, trying to fight her jumbled emotions. She could feel the heat start to smolder between them.

His fingers stroked the smooth flesh of her inner wrist as he wrapped his other hand around the nape of her neck, drawing her face nearer. Mac gave her a long soul-searching stare that tangled all her emotions. "You can tell me about it, you know. That's the good part about ships passing in the night—strangers make good listeners," he said gently, sheltering her against the chilly wind.

"I can't stay here forever."

"Why in the Sam Hill can't you? Whose rules are you taking into account now? Look, take a job if you need to, but I'm asking you to stay."

Diana put her hand on his chest to place some distance between them, and felt the hard beat of his heart beneath her palm. She had to fight to keep herself from responding to his scent, his warmth and those probing eyes.

The wind blew through her hair, causing one strand to brush his lips. His mouth, held in a firm line, softened sensuously as his fingers began to caress the back of her neck. "You're fighting the past," he whispered, his head lowering. "Why don't you let it go?"

Entranced by his slow deep drawl, Diana tilted back her head. His knuckles brushed her breasts, and she felt his lean body grow taut, saw the almost savage flaring of his nostrils.

"Alex called while you were walking." Mac's voice now had a clipped edge to it, as though he didn't want to relay any messages for Alex. "It seems you left the bed-and-breakfast number with your sons. Alex traced you here. He's hot on your trail, isn't he?"

Mac placed both hands on the barn, effectively trapping her. Anger flickered in his eyes.

Diana took a deep steadying breath, feeling Mac's very solid frame warm her. Closing her eyes she inhaled his scent and willed new life into her. She wanted to be rid of her insecurities.

Mac's raw and caring voice whispered urgently into her ear. "Let it go, Diana."

She trembled, fighting the futile desperation that still surfaced in her quiet moments. "Oh, Mac, you don't know—"

"Maybe I do." Placing one finger beneath her chin, he raised her face to his. His mouth brushed hers lightly. "Loving and losing are hard things to do. You're a strong woman, Diana. You wouldn't be here slugging it out with yourself if you weren't."

When she remained silent, he added, "Alex wants you to call him back."

Diana studied Mac's tanned face, trying to see beyond his steady gaze. "Is it about the boys? Are they hurt?"

Mac gently stroked her cheek. "I don't think that's exactly why Alex wanted you to call." He held her tightly for a moment, and then he stepped back, crossing his arms over his chest. "He wants you back, doesn't he?"

"He's not going to get me," Diana answered firmly.

Mac smiled lightly. "Atta girl. I didn't like his remark about us shacking up together very well myself."

Diana's eyes widened. "Did he say that?" Fierce anger was suddenly coursing hotly through her.

Mac pushed the Stetson back from his face, and a strand of black hair fell across his dark forehead. "Not exactly in those terms."

"Oh, I see. The famous 'man talk' that can't be repeated in front of females," she snapped.

Mac's lean cheeks darkened with a flush. "Something like that. Are you going to call him back? He's worried about your reputation. Nettled as hell about you staying with me. Seems that Ray put in a word or two about us getting married. We had quite a conversation. He wanted me to tuck you in your station wagon and send you home."

"What did you say?"

Mac's head tilted, the brim of the Stetson shadowing his eyes. "I invited him to drop by and do it himself."

"And?"

"He said he just might do that."

Diana felt anger slicing through her like a hot knife. Alex deserved to get back a little of his own, and she suddenly found advantages to Mac's game.

Without pressing her, Mac had given her back her self-esteem as a woman. He had gently reawakened her femininity, and she'd needed that to feel complete.

She could feel her heels dig deeper in the mud, as though she were settled in for a good fight. She knew she could support herself financially, but there were other areas where the wounds still hadn't completely healed. If Alex needed to see her surviving, so be it. She'd spread her newfound confidence all over his leering face. Because she *knew* what she was: a desirable woman.

Desirable. The word lingered as she thought of Mac's large hand sweeping gently down her body, his fingers trembling. His rough cheeks had heated and colored, and his black eyes had flickered with need for her kiss.

She slyly glanced at Mac's broad shoulders and height. He was as virile as a man could be, and he had wanted her. Mac was absolute proof that she had all the appeal a woman needed.

Alex needed to be taught a lesson. If he had to have the complete picture drawn for him, Diana knew that Mac would comply. Alex would have to look hard and long at the new Diana to find his "house mouse."

On the other hand, Alex wasn't really worth it.

But when Mac added softly, "Seems he can't see you forging out a life in the wilderness—without the Cadillac and his credit cards," Diana felt defiance blazing anew within her.

"Revenge can be sweet. I'm game, how about you?" Mac asked, grinning widely.

"Uh-huh," she responded. She felt like cutting all her restrictive ties to the past. With her home leased for one year and her two sons spending Thanksgiving with Alex, there was absolutely no reason she couldn't stay longer. "I've been thinking that I may stay more than a week, Mac. You wouldn't mind having a Rayfield Inn leftover for some extra days, would you?"

He shook his head. "Just for the hell of it?"

"For the sheer hell of it," she corrected. "I didn't have a thing planned past this week in Benevolence."

"Ah, there's nothing like a woman who's steamed up," Mac teased. "Suits me. I'm enjoying myself."

"Oh, so am I," she stated, knowing it was true.

They began walking toward the house. "If we're going to set up...housekeeping, we'd better buy a few things to get tongues wagging, don't you think?" Diana asked.

When Mac didn't answer, she turned sharply, catching his gaze on her hips. Diana's confidence fluttered and soared. It was really nice to have Mac around; he did wonders for her spirit. She was having a really good time now.

Mac leaned against the counter, feeling embarrassed at being in the women's lingerie section of the dry goods store. He glanced at the hunting supply section and caught Neil Wingman smirking behind aluminum tent poles. Deciding that the store owner could go to blazes, Mac gazed back at Diana.

Her slender back was up, it seemed. She'd latched on to Mac's arm the minute she'd stepped out of the pickup in downtown Benevolence. Every beaming smile was focused so brightly on him that he'd begun to sweat beneath his shearling coat. She'd tossed so many "honeys" and "sweethearts" and adoring looks at him that he was starting to feel like a real fiancé.

He was also starting to feel as possessive as a real fiancé, he realized slowly. If they were really going to get married... Mac stopped in midthought as Diana's delicate hands smoothed out a lacy black confection.

When she said, "Oh, look, Mac. Isn't it nice?" Wingman let out a snicker.

Mac, incensed that two customers were leering at Diana, tightened his fists. In another minute he'd have to politely ask all three men outside to preserve Diana's honor. "Diana, this section is for the—" he paused, his face heating "—the party set. It's a joke in a store like this. That thing is X-rated. Put it down."

Wingman laughed out loud, and Mac took just one threatening step toward the man before Diana's hand on his belly stopped him. He glanced down and found her looking at him through her lashes so seductively, so sensually promising, that he felt as though his boots were stuck to the wooden floor. His breath caught in his dry throat, and his male impulses told him to sweep her into his arms and taste that sweet petal-soft mouth. If they were married, he'd take her on home . . .

"What is wrong with you?" she demanded sharply through gritted teeth, still smiling. "You look as though someone snatched a piece of pie away from you. Stop it. We're creating an image, remember?"

She held the black teddy against her body, modeling the skimpy garment for him. "Mac?" she persisted, the sensuous look deepening. "You could act as though you like it. There's more to this game than just living together, you know. Even I know that."

Mac's gaze drifted over the teddy and her curves behind it. Mac could feel the wild throbbing within him, the primitive need to claim her and have her body beneath him.

He groaned inwardly, thrusting his fists into his jeans pockets. Diana needed time to sort out her problems; she didn't need him acting like a bull elk at mating season. To cover his desire, he spoke roughly. "Looks fine. Put it on my bill."

Diana's fine eyebrows lifted. "I will not. I'm quite capable of paying my own bills."

"Men are supposed to buy their ladies things like—that." He nodded at the wispy garment, hearing Wingman snicker again.

"Times have changed, Mac," Diana stated tightly.

"Better back up, boy," the storekeeper offered, moving toward them.

Mac shot him a look that could have melted lead and turned back to Diana, his jaw taut. "Get used to it, Diana. As long as you're in Benevolence, I'm footing the bill."

Her slender fingers crushed the teddy; her eyes darkened. "Says who?"

"Lovers' tiff?" Wingman teased, approaching them. "Say, I heard you two were getting married. Short notice, isn't it? How did you meet?"

"My brother Rafe introduced us last year. I've been expecting her," Mac said. She was his to take care of, wasn't she? That meant paying her bills.

"Rafe can pick 'em. So she's staying with you?" Wingman's gaze narrowed on Diana's petite body, appraising her slender build right down to her shoes. Mac took a deep breath, held it to the count of ten and slowly wrapped his arm around her shoulders, drawing her next to him.

Acting like Diana's possessive future husband wasn't difficult, he discovered. "She's getting the place in shape. You know, measuring things," Mac explained while pressing a kiss to her temple.

The sweet scent of her hair intoxicated him, and he found himself closing his eyes, barely breathing, wishing that they were alone on the mesa. She looked as pretty as a cluster of snow buttercups breaking the winter snow.

Diana shifted away, her face averted. "Mac's right. We're getting the house ready before I look for work."

"Hmm. Work." Wingman scratched his jaw. "I'll be needing someone to help me with the paperwork after a week. My clerk, Andrea, is quitting to stay home with her kids. What do you think? Just part-time, enough to keep the receipts straight for the accountant. Some ordering stuff.''

"I'd like that—'' Diana began.

"Diana has enough to do at the house," Mac said firmly, determined to keep her close to him as much as possible. He didn't know how long she was staying, and he couldn't stop her from leaving when she felt it was time to go. So for now while she was here, he would make sure she stayed beside him.

"Huh!" Wingman snorted. "I've known you for a long time, Mac. Never figured you to stop a woman from working if she wanted to. Funny, you hermits have weird ideas about women—once you finally trap one."

Wingman winked at Diana, who boldly returned the gesture. "She's got that soft look, Mac," he observed thoughtfully. "Like Eleanor, but different, you know? Diana looks like she might like taking a wilderness survival trip up on old Smokey."

He laughed, watching Mac begin to simmer. "Boy, you MacLean boys are slow to get riled, but now we've got you."

Diana's arm slipped around Mac's waist. She pinched him just once, but hard enough to make him wince. "We can have the place in shape in two weeks, Mac. Besides, he said only part-time."

Standing on tiptoe, she reached up and kissed his cheek. "Shut up or you'll never get another loaf of homemade bread," she whispered urgently. "Or berry pie."

Still leaning against Mac, Diana smiled at Wingman. "We'll talk it over, and I'll give you a call. I don't see anything wrong with part-time work, at least through the holidays. Would that be okay, for now?''

"I'll take whatever hours you can give me and appreciate 'em," Wingman answered heartily. "When things settle down for you two, we might work out something else.''

Later, Mac followed Diana through the grocery store, pushing the laden cart. Actually he enjoyed shopping with her, watching her study the different brands intently before choosing one and placing it in the cart. He missed shopping with a woman.

Diana struggled with a twenty-five-pound sack of flour. He lifted it into the cart for her. "Are you sure you need this much?''

Her eyes blazed; she looked furious. "Are you always going to question my needs? I'm good and mad, Mac. And when I'm mad, I bake," she stated, placing a bottle of vanilla in the cart.

"What's wrong?''

"Let's just say I had different plans for my little sabbatical from reality. I hadn't planned to be a prisoner in your house when I agreed to this farce. I didn't like your domineering noises at the store. *I* want to work at Wingman's.''

Mac studied his hands on the handle of the cart. "The outfitter's is a man's hangout, Diana. For hunting guides and their customers," he said carefully, uncertain as to her reaction. "The language gets rough in there sometimes. Ah, colorful, you know.''

"I raised two sons, Mac. I haven't been all that sheltered." Then she looked at him carefully. "Are you blushing?''

"Hell, no. I'm just saying that Wingman's is okay, but—"

"I can handle myself, Mac. You can't do it for me," Diana stated softly, placing a hand on his cheek. "You're hot. You *are* blushing," she asserted.

"I haven't had a lot of practice at this," Mac said. "Anything could happen to you. What I mean is, you're just getting your bearings. Don't dive in head-first."

"You said I was strong, Mac." Diana's fingers explored the crease between his thick brows. "Don't you see? While we're playing at this—" she lowered her voice "—engagement, I have some very serious thinking to do. I'm questioning my past, building foundations for the future. Do you understand? Didn't you go through that when you lost your wife?"

"I went through a lot," Mac said, looking at the huge gunnysack of potatoes to avoid Diana's searching gaze. "Eleanor shouldn't have been out in that blizzard, helping me feed cattle. She never fully recovered from pneumonia."

"I know. And you're hurting just like me, right?" Her gentle tone made him look up, and he saw her concerned expression. "I did hurt plenty. Then I shut the door. It was that or go crazy." Mac felt his heart miss a beat when her hand rested on the side of his neck.

Mac swallowed as she caressed his cheek. He didn't want the pain of loving and losing again, the happiness now, then the ripping of heart and soul later. . . .

"And you play bagpipes at midnight. Oh, Mac," Diana murmured. "You look so sad."

He thought he heard her sigh, and his gaze strayed down to her lips and lingered there. When he saw her tongue flick moisture on them, it was all he could do to reach out and pull her into his arms.

It had been so long. . . .

Her dark eyes shone brightly beneath her lashes. "I'll be your friend, Mac," she stated unevenly.

After a moment, he smiled. "Friend. That's nice."

The next morning, Diana was shaping bread dough just as Mac padded into the kitchen.

He mumbled a halfhearted greeting, his stockinged feet locked on a path to the coffeepot. In the light of dawn passing through the windows, Diana could see the line of dark hair trailing down from his bare chest to below that open first snap of his jeans. A pale strip of flesh showed above the waistband. Totally entranced, she stopped working on the dough.

Mac turned his back—a rippling, intriguing back—to pour coffee into a mug. He had such a nice physique—broad shoulders, lean waist and narrow hips. The worn jeans clung to his firm buttocks, the back pocket faded from his wallet.

Cup of coffee in hand, he made his way toward the table. He sat, staring at the dark liquid as though it could solve the world's problems. Sleepy and rumpled, Mac had a totally lovable look about him, and Diana found her thoughts returning to the woman he had loved. Wingman had said Eleanor had a "soft" look.

Mac needed a soft woman, she decided.

"Good morning, sleepyhead." She placed the dough in the pans, oiled the top of the loaves and put them aside to rise. "You're up early."

"It's hard to sleep with pots and pans clanging in the middle of the night," he grumbled. He surveyed the kitchen counter, covered with platters of brownies and cookies. "You've been busy. We can't eat all that."

"I thought you could take some over to that nice Mr. Clancy. He's promised to teach me how to mush."

Mac glared up at her. "That old codger isn't getting all of it."

"I have cookie dough in the refrigerator. There will be plenty." Diana wiped her hands on the towel serving as her apron. She'd had a bad night, the cold small bed plaguing her sleep. Eventually, she'd wrapped the blanket around her and spent the night on the couch, snuggling against the back.

In the twilight hours, she seemed to be defenseless against the nagging emptiness. Was that the reason people took lovers—to fill the empty nights? At her age, how could a second love be as exciting and demanding as the first passion?

She couldn't spend her life baking and cleaning nooks and crannies. At the moment, she could only think of baiting Mac—a sport she had come to enjoy. "Someone tried to play bagpipes out in the barn last night."

Over the rim of his cup, his eyes widened almost comically. "Tried? Those cows like my midnight serenades. I'll have you know..." He paused as she slid a platter of bacon, eggs and hash brown potatoes in front of him. His eyes lighted up, and he grinned up at her. "Mmm."

After a moment he turned serious, rubbing the stubble covering his jaw. "I didn't sleep well," he said, looking intently at her. "I came down at two o'clock and found you on the couch."

"You worked on your plans." She could feel Mac's gaze stripping her, probing her emotions. Uncomfortable at his scrutiny, she turned to the window to watch the pink dawn rise over the sawtooth-shaped mountaintops. In the stillness of the night, the sounds he'd made—the rustling of paper, the creaking of his chair, his talking quietly on the radio—had made her feel safe. They'd wrapped around her like a down comforter, and gradually she had slipped into a deep sleep.

She looked back at him. "What are you doing today?" she asked, trying to change the flow of her thoughts.

"I'm going out in the copter the first thing this morning," he said. "There's sign of poachers up on the Ewing Mesa. They've butchered five or six deer for bait."

She glanced outside and saw clouds hovering low on the mountains. "I want to go." Diana smiled to herself, slightly surprised by her demand.

"You can't." He put a forkful of potatoes into his mouth. "This is really good."

Diana grabbed his plate from him and held it aloft. "I want to go, Mac," she insisted.

His jaw jutted out pugnaciously. His hand ran through his sleek black hair, mussing it up in a way that made him look lovable. "No way. We'll go joyriding some other time. I promised the game warden I'd look for signs of poachers today and bring back any information."

Diana walked to Red's food bowl and lowered Mac's plate near it, threatening him silently.

"Okay, you can go," he agreed reluctantly, eyeing Red's alert stance. "But at the first sign of trouble, I'm bringing you home."

"Why?" she demanded sharply.

"You could get hurt," he replied between his teeth as he rose to walk toward her. "Poachers don't like to get caught, you know. Once in a while they take a potshot at the copters. . . ." His eyes narrowed. "For some reason, you get feisty in the morning, while I'm still trying to wake up."

"If you wouldn't spend all night hunched over a drawing board, you'd feel better in the mornings."

"Look who's talking." For a moment his dark eyes searched hers. A lock of hair fell across his forehead. "You sleep better when you're lying up against something...someone, Diana," he murmured. "You're the kind of woman who needs cuddling."

Diana could feel the heat from his body, almost feel the springy hair covering his chest. She backed up against the counter, still holding the plate. Mac placed his hands on her hips, looming over her. Elemental heat waves surged between them as he asked, "When are we getting married, friend?"

He took the plate from her and placed it on the counter, then inched closer to her. Mac stared at her mouth like a starved man, his chest nearing her hot cheek. "Just to answer the town's questions. You know, if we were really getting married, last night could have been better for both of us.''

His low husky drawl sent tingly sparks up her spine. ''We could...'' Mac's lips brushed her temple.

Unsteadily, Diana placed her palms against his chest and felt his muscles tighten in response to her touch. ''I've been in that Mother Goose fairy tale—it didn't work. Let me go.''

His jaw hardened, his eyes flashed. ''Lady, someday you'll trust me. You'll jump off that high wall and find yourself in one piece, not broken up like Humpty Dumpty.''

She forced a small space between them. How could he be so sure when she was so scared? *''All the king's horses and all the king's men, couldn't put Humpty together again.''* ''You're pushing, Mac.''

He toyed with a curl just behind her ear, studying the reddish tint in the light of dawn. ''Could be. I've been out of practice so long, I'm not certain. I just know that I like your perfume, the way the bathroom feels all rosy when you step out of it. A man misses those things, you know. The little things like a dainty lace bra drying over the shower rod, that sort of thing.''

''That's not enough.'' She could have told him about the emptiness then, but somehow she thought he knew. Involuntarily, her hands slid over the smooth planes of his shoulders, exploring, feeling...

''You're afraid of me, aren't you, Mac?'' The men she'd known had always seemed so sure of themselves, demanding and taking.

"I'd be a fool not to be. I've been to hell and back, and I wouldn't care to repeat the experience. You're the first one to hear that."

He shifted slightly, the movement bringing his hips against hers. "God, you're soft." He nuzzled her neck. "Mmm, you smell like bread dough."

She giggled, trusting him enough to let him touch her. It had been so long since she'd trusted a man that much. Mac's mouth slid along her jawline, his breath swirling around her hot cheek.

Diana barely breathed, enjoying the light scrape of his beard. Allowing her hands to drift to his waist, she looped her fingers through his belt. "Mr. MacLean, do you know what you're doing?"

"Stirring things up?" he asked huskily against her lips, teasing them with tiny kisses.

She trembled, wanting to run her palms over the smoothness of his back. The need to open her mouth to his became so strong that she gasped. Closing her eyes, Diana wondered about the intense emotions racing through her. "Too much, Mac," she murmured, moving away.

He stared at her, his eyes heavy lidded with desire. "Mmm?"

"Friends don't act like this, Mac," she began, fretting with her needs and her denials, looking away.

His warm knuckles grazed her soft cheek. "Of course they do," he returned gently, pulling her into his arms.

For a long moment, he just held her. "Yesterday is gone, Diana."

Five

Yesterday is gone. A week later, Diana repeated the words, liking the sound of them.

Seated next to Mac in the soaring helicopter, she surveyed the snow-covered buttes and the pine forests below. She adjusted the headphones he had insisted she wear. Above the valley a golden eagle soared, his huge brown wings glistening in the sun. Her eyes following him, Diana felt a kinship with the bird in his lonely flight.

The craggy panorama contrasted with Missouri's rounded hills and oaks as much as her sons' temperaments differed. Rick, a college freshmen, was dependable and even tempered, while Blaine lived for the moment.

Diana felt a pain sweep through her, and she closed her eyes. The breach between her sons and herself—

caused by the divorce—remained despite her efforts. And this "vacation" was only deepening it. She remembered how upset her sons were when she'd told them about it. They hadn't said it, but she'd known they felt she was abandoning them. When she'd called Rick at his college dorm to give him Mac's phone number, she'd suffered at the coldness in his voice. He hadn't even asked how she was.

Maybe Mac's "game" wasn't so harmless. Maybe she should pack up her things, drive to Missouri and try to patch up her marriage.... Go back to being a "house mouse"? Go back to Alex? Never! She'd find some other way of winning back her sons.

Mac broke into her thoughts by pointing out a mountain goat, who was watching them from a mountain ledge. With agile certainty, the goat leaped down and disappeared into a stand of blue spruce trees. "Slumgullion Pass is over that way, and Wagon Wheel Gap is over there."

Mac tilted the helicopter to follow a high mountain trail. Scanning a creek, he frowned. "Four-wheelers tearing up the ground," he noted. "Looks like they had a private party out here sometime this week. See that bonfire?"

"How do you know it was this week?"

"I've been prowling this mountain every few days since the poaching started. Those tracks weren't there last week."

A black bear lumbered out into a small clearing, saw the helicopter and returned to the forest. "Look over there," Mac ordered briskly. "See where they crossed that gravel bar? They're running traps, baiting for wolf and cat. Looks like they've been cutting some federal timber, too. Probably selling it for fire-wood—the government won't like that."

They scanned the gorges and mesas for the next hour, Mac speaking briefly to point out old mines and logging camps. He pointed to a ski lift strung be-tween two peaks and chuckled. "I had to rescue some young lovers stranded between stations once. They never even noticed the blizzard until it was too late. Named their first child after me."

Diana nodded, enjoying the scenic beauty, aware of Mac's deep love for the rugged country.

He nodded toward an awesome sheer rock bluff that faced a rugged pine-studded mountain. A narrow passage separated the two. The helicopter swooped to the right, then dived straight for the passage.

"Mac!" Holding her breath, Diana closed her eyes and reached out to grip Mac's arm. Immediately the helicopter paused.

Diana opened one eye and saw Mac's wide grin. She looked around and realized they were hovering in the passage. "I want to live," she enunciated carefully. "That trick could have cost our lives."

He nodded, unconcerned. "True. But I've flown this spot for years." Then he pointed to his lips. "Don't I get one right here for my expertise and keeping you alive?"

Her eyes widened, the beat of her heart pounding in her ears. "What?"

He winked, his face lighting up with laughter. "I want a smooch from my best girl."

"Mac," she protested hotly, staring down the sev-eral hundred feet to the earth. "This is dangerous."

"Only if I don't get my kiss." The helicopter dipped abruptly, causing Diana to inhale sharply. Mac stared at her pale face, his grin drying. "Okay, then. I'll settle for a whopper on the ground."

The helicopter flew through the passage and headed home.

After landing, Mac unbuckled Diana's safety belt and eased her shaking legs to the solid safe earth. Her eyes were closed. When her knees buckled, he gripped her jacket collar with both his hands and leaned her against him, supporting her weight easily.

"Hey, I didn't mean to scare you that bad," he murmured. She kept her lids firmly closed. "Knock, knock. Is anyone in there?"

"I'm really mad, Mac." Though she tried, she couldn't unwrap her fingers from his strong secure wrists.

"No sense of humor," he accused. "You weren't in any danger."

Diana forced open one eye, comforted to see the pine branches above her head now. A cold mist tingled on her face. "I could kill you," she managed to say quietly, despite the anger churning within her. She was a volcano about to erupt.

"There's nothing like good honest emotion," Mac assured her. "You've been taking out your anger on that damned dough and by cleaning everything in sight. I've had to hang out wash just to get to talk to you," he said quietly, watching the color slowly return to her face. "I'll bet you've had plenty of practice hiding your emotions. In fact, you probably just waltzed around any unpleasantries, right?"

When she glared at him, he continued, "You've been brooding about your family. You've picked up the phone and put it down too many times. You've written, but no one is returning the letters. Come on, admit it. Let it out," he urged harshly. "I'm here—try it all out on me." He held on to her hips.

He'd run his scalpel too close to her emotional marrow, exposing her frustrations. He had no right to probe and push and enter her private arena of pain. She didn't owe him anything. It was he who owed her for agreeing to play along with his game.

She breathed hard, fighting back the tears. "Let me go. I'm leaving."

Mac pressed his face against hers. "That's right, run off. Find someplace else to lick your wounds. Clean the whole mountainside, for all I care. Dust the barn. Dust the pines. Reality is right here and now, Diana. I thought you had decided to fight for it. But the first time I come too close, you're ready to turn tail."

"You can't possibly know my problems. That's unfair," she insisted, throwing back her head. The wind whipped her hair around her face.

"Of course, it is. Who said life was fair?" Mac wanted to rip her free from her past and help her put together a new life. "You've still got a whole life left. How are you going to live it?" he demanded, wondering about his life and the emptiness surrounding him before Diana's arrival.

She dashed a hand across her cheek, wiping away a tear.

He hated himself for hurting her. "Call your sons, Diana," he murmured, kissing her damp lashes and feeling the tenseness of her body. "Invite them here, if you want. We've got plenty of room."

We, he repeated silently to himself. Somehow in less than two weeks, he had come to think of his house as Diana's home. He'd frightened her when he'd asked her to marry him. Hell, he'd frightened himself. He didn't mean it—or did he?

Ordinarily, he wasn't a pushy man. He'd always let a stray choose its own way. Only this stray had big velvety eyes in a pale face, sweet vulnerable lips and caused him to start feeling he was a kid again.

Or a man about to fall off a very safe, very lonely mountain. She wasn't exactly thrilled about the idea, either.

He took a deep breath, trying to get his bearings. While he held Diana's body close, his thumbs rubbing her hips, everything inside him seemed to heat up. Pressed against his chest, her soft breasts were so enticing. He shuddered with the need to hold them in his hands.

Mac began to breathe heavily. "I never got my kiss," he whispered unsteadily.

"You're deliberately keeping me off balance." Diana lowered her gaze.

Enchanted by the tiny vein throbbing beneath the satin skin of her neck, Mac bent to place his lips on that exact spot. He liked tasting Diana, feeling her slender body tense in his arms, hearing her slight gasp.

Her head turned, her parted lips brushing his somehow. An explosion of ecstasy inside him caused Mac to forget everything but the woman in his arms.

```
**************************************************
* You may have already won a lifetime of cash payments *
* totaling up to $1,000,000.00!  Play our Sweepstakes *
* Game--Here's how it works...                     *
**************************************************
```

Each of the first three tickets has a unique Sweepstakes number.
If your Sweepstakes numbers match any of the winning numbers
selected by our computer, you could win the amount shown under
the gold rub-off on that ticket.

Using an eraser, rub off the gold boxes on tickets #1-3 to
reveal how much each ticket could be worth if it is a winning
ticket. You must return the _entire_ card to be eligible. (See
official rules in the back of this book for details.)

At the same time you play your tickets for big cash prizes,
Silhouette also invites you to participate in a special trial of
our Reader Service by accepting one or more FREE book(s) from
Silhouette Desire.® To request your free book(s), just rub off
the gold box on ticket #4 to reveal how many free book(s) you
will receive.

When you receive your free book(s), we hope you'll enjoy them
and want to see more. So unless we hear from you, every month
we'll send you 6 additional Silhouette Desire®novels. Each book
is yours to keep for only $2.24* each--26¢ less per book than
the cover price! There are _no_ additional charges for shipping
and handling and of course, you may cancel Reader Service
privileges at any time by marking "cancel" on your shipping
statement or returning an unopened shipment of books to us at
our expense. Either way your shipments will stop. You'll
receive no more books; you'll have no further obligation.

PLUS-you get a FREE MYSTERY GIFT!

If you return your game card with **all four gold boxes** rubbed
off, you will also receive a FREE Mystery Gift. It's your
immediate reward for sampling your free book(s), **and** it's yours
to keep no matter what you decide.

P.S.

Remember, the first set of one or more book(s) is FREE. So rub
off the gold box on ticket #4 and return the entire sheet of
tickets today!

*Terms and prices subject to change without notice.
 Sales taxes applicable in New York and Iowa.

"GIVE YOUR HEART TO SILHOUETTE" SWEEPSTAKES

DETACH HERE AND RETURN ENTIRE SHEET OF TICKETS NOW!

#1

$1,000,000.00

Rub off to reveal potential value if this is a winning ticket: ►

UNIQUE SWEEPSTAKES NUMBER: 6B   523544

#2

$1,000,000.00

Rub off to reveal potential value if this is a winning ticket: ►

UNIQUE SWEEPSTAKES NUMBER: 7B   525529

#3

$1,000,000.00

Rub off to reveal potential value if this is a winning ticket: ►

UNIQUE SWEEPSTAKES NUMBER: 8B   523195

#4

ONE OR MORE FREE BOOKS

HOW MANY FREE BOOKS?
Rub off to reveal number of free books you will receive ►

1672765559

Yes! Enter my sweepstakes numbers in the Sweepstakes and let me know if I've won a cash prize. If gold box on ticket #4 is rubbed off, I will also receive one or more Silhouette Desire® novels as a FREE tryout of the Reader Service, along with a FREE Mystery Gift as explained on the opposite page.

225 CIS JAYY

NAME

ADDRESS   APT.

CITY   STATE   ZIP CODE

Offer not valid to current Silhouette Desire® subscribers. All orders subject to approval.   PRINTED IN U.S.A.

DON'T FORGET...

... Return this card today with ticket #4 rubbed off, and receive 4 free books and a free mystery gift.

... You will receive books well before they're available in stores and at a discount off cover prices.

... No obligation to buy. You can cancel at any time by writing "cancel" on your statement or returning an unopened shipment to us at our cost.

BUSINESS REPLY CARD

First Class   Permit No. 717   Buffalo, NY

Postage will be paid by addressee

Silhouette Reader Service ™

MILLION DOLLAR SWEEPSTAKES
901 Fuhrmann Blvd.
P.O. Box 1867
Buffalo, N.Y. 14240-9952

NO POSTAGE
NECESSARY
IF MAILED
IN THE
UNITED STATES

Her fingers slowly tangled in his hair. She tilted her head, looking directly into his eyes. "Do you know what you're doing?"

"I think so," he whispered, marveling at her beauty.

"We shouldn't be doing this." Her fingers slid across his brows, smoothing them. The caress trailed down his nose, causing Mac's breath to halt. He exhaled slowly as her cheek rubbed his.

"What else are friends for?" He caught the delicate lobe of her ear between his teeth, tugging it gently. *Friends?* Who was he kidding?

Diana's touch trailed down his jaw to his throat, her eyes following the glide of her slender fingers over his dark skin. Slowly, she unbuttoned his shirt, exposing his chest. "You have a . . . nice chest," she said, staring at it solemnly.

"Thank you. So do you." Lord, he loved those small inquisitive fingers caressing his flesh.

A flush rose from her neck, and suddenly Mac realized how very innocent she was, despite her marriage.

"How do you know?" she asked breathlessly. She lowered her cheek to rub it against the hair at the base of his neck.

"I guessed." Mac closed his eyes, fighting the throbbing need that had begun to course through him. She trailed kisses across his left shoulder, her fingers tugging his shirt aside. One fingertip prowled around his left nipple, raising a helpless groan from Mac. "You're not being fair, Diana."

His hands cupped her derriere. He tried to read her thoughtful expression. "Are we using good old Mac as an experiment, Diana?'' he asked, giving in to the urge to kiss that delicious bottom lip.

She mulled the thought over, looking out into the fields. "It's the middle of the day, Mac. Someone could drive past."

"So? I thought that was the image you wanted to spread around Benevolence." He closed his eyes, envisioning holding her without the barrier of clothing.

"You're aroused," she whispered huskily, her fingers splayed across his chest, toying with the hair.

"Mmm, slightly." Mac wanted to rip off their clothes and unleash his passion. But he also wanted to be tender and take away all her pain. . . .

She shifted her hips and he groaned, aware that his blood had begun to throb hotly. Taking a deep shuddering breath, he pressed his face into her collar, finding the delicate curve of her throat. Her satin-smooth flesh was so warm beneath his open lips.

Diana's arms locked around his neck. "Mac."

He opened the top buttons on her shirt to reveal the gentle slopes of her breasts. He stared hungrily. He could almost feel their weight—

"Mac," she protested more sharply, drawing her shirt closed with one hand. She squirmed, pushing him until his arms were empty. "Don't."

Gazing up at him solemnly, Diana whispered something, her face hot.

Dazed, wanting to pull her back into his arms, Mac found the strength to ask, "What?"

She looked at Old Bob rubbing his shoulder against the feedlot fence. "I'm sorry. You've been so kind. . . ."

Mac felt confused. Where had they been? Where were they going? "I don't get it."

Diana's sad eyes looked away from his piercing ones. "You wouldn't. I know you're trying your best to help me over this rough spot...."

Mac swallowed, feeling the warm moment crumble. Standing guiltily before him, Diana clumsily tried to button her shirt. She looked as though she'd been found out.

"I'm all tangled up inside," she said quietly, her slender fingers twitching, as though seeking a lifeline to hold on to. Mac remained silent, knowing that she needed time to form her thoughts into words.

There was so much aching in her eyes when she looked up at him—those wounded eyes. "We were married for twenty years—a lifetime, Mac. It's difficult to explain."

Mac felt the chill of the November wind right down to his bones. "Don't you think you should stop mourning?" he asked softly as he brushed a strand of hair back from her cheek.

"I couldn't just jump into the dating arena, Mac. I'm not built that way." Her eyes darkened, meeting his. "Have you stopped hurting?" she questioned in return, the husky whisper almost knocking him against the fence.

Mac framed her delicate jaw with his hands. He felt his reluctant wistful smile right down to his boots. "Lately, it's been easier."

Sleeping wasn't easy, Mac finally admitted to himself at one o'clock the next morning. In fact, with Diana tossing and turning on her creaky bed, he couldn't sleep at all. So he'd come out to the living room to work but found he couldn't concentrate, either. He leaned back in his chair, staring at the blueprints for the electrical panels, which he'd been doing for an hour.

He scratched his bare chest, remembering once more the sight of her breasts. He groaned. A strong feeling of restlessness was pulsing in his body. It was a tightening, a sensual energy that he hadn't known for years.

He caught her scent, heard her clothing rustle before her hand rested lightly on his shoulder. The sleeve of her robe brushed his jaw. "Mac?" She leaned closer, her eyes huge and luminous and showing incredible tenderness. "What are you doing, Mac?" she asked.

He couldn't say, "Fighting to keep away from you." He couldn't say, "I need you, Diana."

"Mac?" she persisted, massaging his shoulders. "You're tired. Go on to bed."

Diana's touch soothed his aching muscles and Mac closed his eyes. Without thinking, he allowed his hand to settle on her waist, as though it had that right. She tensed as his hand followed the rounded curve of her hip in a slow caress. "Will you tuck me in?"

She laughed. "You're hardly Rick or Blaine."

The moment of intimacy lingered and grew as she stood still beneath his hand, trusting him. Mac wondered if she knew her breast almost brushed his cheek. He closed his eyes and rested his head upon the slight mound. The feeling of rightness settled around Mac like a cozy comforter on a cold, cold night.

Diana tensed, breathing lightly. Her hand stilled upon his shoulder. Her fingers touched his hair for just a fraction of a second, then lifted. "I can't stay, Mac," she stated huskily.

Mac couldn't think of anything that would take Diana from him. He turned slightly to see her face better. The movement pushed her robe aside and brought his rough cheek sliding against her bare softness.

Neither moved, the room suddenly washed with emotions.

"Mac," she protested on a soft, soft whisper. "Don't."

His lips brushed the fragrant bare flesh, the softness luring him. She gasped when his mouth touched the sensitive crest of her breast.

"Oh, Mac," she moaned, her fingers tightening on his hair. "I'm not too sure about this."

The old house creaked, protesting the rising winter wind. Outside it was cold, but here inside the house, Mac could feel the fiery blaze within him. His senses were filled with Diana, and he trembled when he felt her heart thumping wildly beneath his cheek.

Mac wanted her. He fought the desire to carry her to his bed and claim her. But that pleasure would only be fleeting. With Diana, he wanted more.

Wrapping both arms around Diana's small waist, Mac pulled her between his knees. She was holding her robe closed now, her eyes glistening with tears, her cheeks flushed.

Diana had her ghosts and he had his, he decided, pulling her down to his lap. "Midnight is a good time to talk, Diana,'' he murmured, easing her head onto his shoulder.

She caught his wrist and pressed his palm to her cheek. Cradling the delicate bones of her face, Mac waited. He sensed Diana had to take her own time.

Still holding his wrist, Diana guided his hand to the softness beneath her robe. ''What are you doing now, Diana?'' he asked carefully, feeling the soft flesh quiver beneath his palm.

She leaned against his shoulder, her eyes guarded by the shadows of her lashes. ''I . . . wanted to see how it would feel . . . again.''

Mac traced the full vulnerable line of her parted lips and kissed her lightly. ''And?''

She looked up at him. ''I think you're a gentle man, Mac.''

With his hand resting on her flesh, Mac didn't feel gentle. He felt like a leashed wild man. Her fingers caressed his brows and cheekbones, and he closed his lids, savoring her butterfly-light touch. ''Well, there comes a point for any man, honey . . .''

''Not you,'' Diana returned firmly, smoothing his fierce brows with her thumb. She shifted on Mac's lap, needing his arms wrapped around her. She'd run so fast and so hard, protecting her emotions and trying to begin her new life, that there had been no time. ''It gets lonely, doesn't it, Mac?''

''Sure does, honey,'' he agreed roughly. She felt the trembling of his hand as his fingers splayed across her chest. He wouldn't hurt her.

Diana studied the tense craggy face with the evening's growth of beard. ''I feel as though I'm in a time warp, and I'm back where I was twenty years ago.''

Would he laugh? Somehow, she knew he understood.

"The rules changed, didn't they?"

She nodded slowly, enjoying the feel of his hard chest beneath her palm. She loved to touch Mac.

His warm hand slid to her other breast, cradling it tenderly. "We are friends, aren't we?"

His thumb slid across the very tip of her breast, the touch striking unfamiliar cords within Diana's body. "We're the best of friends."

Diana rested her fingertips on his throat and felt his pulse beating heavily there. He swallowed, then gasped, making her look up at his tense features. "Mac?"

He shifted her and stretched his long legs out from under the desk. He smiled tightly. "Just getting comfortable."

Diana noted the flush on his dark cheeks. "I'm not a girl any longer, Mac," she said carefully, trying out her new emotions, ones that she'd kept locked inside her.

"No, you definitely aren't." He breathed deeply, shifting her on his lap once more. Closing his eyes and leaning his head back against the wall, he placed a hand on her exposed thigh. She found the heavy warmth comforting.

Diana finally felt at peace.

Mac began caressing her thigh, and she watched his tanned hand moving over her pale skin. She noticed that the back of his broad hand bore a sprinkling of black hair, and she pictured his entire body, comparing it to her own.

"I have stretch marks, Mac," she admitted baldly before realizing she had spoken. Would he find her body ugly?

His hand stopped momentarily before continuing the caress. "I have a scar or two myself."

What would Mac expect from her as a lover? Should she touch him first? Diana shivered, surprised by her own questions. She hadn't consciously thought about her needs as a woman for years. Now she realized she'd hidden those innermost emotions, protected her vulnerability. "I have no idea what happens now, Mac," she blurted out.

He tensed and opened his eyes. "You know, neither do I. And somehow, I don't think we should worry about it, at least not tonight."

Diana sat upright, watching him intently. Mac met her gaze steadily, and she sensed the strong currents running between them. "You worry too much, woman," he said finally, brushing her lips with his.

Tracing his bottom lip with her fingertip, Diana trembled. "I don't think I can ever give myself to another man, Mac," she confessed, thinking how very familiar Mac had become to her.

The thought of his lean naked body pressing against hers, demanding, sent off warning rockets in her mind. She couldn't possibly use poor Mac for her guinea pig! To see if she could wipe away her inhibitions and fly with him? Impossible! Mac deserved better.

"I'm too old to start anything now," she murmured to herself as she stood up from his lap. With trembling fingers, she straightened her robe.

"That's what you think," he said softly, his eyes flickering beneath his lashes.

Diana's knees went weak at his hot look. She could feel his desire wrap around her and her own answering need. Abruptly she turned around and almost fled to her room. She ordered herself to close the door without looking back.

Her hand slid to her throat, covering the rapid pulse beating there. Mac deserved nothing but a whole woman in his bed to love him. She was still trying to fit the pieces of her life together. And she'd already had her chance for happiness.

Hadn't she?

Six

Mac turned over on his rumpled bed for the fiftieth time and glanced at his bedside clock. "Three o'clock," he muttered disbelievingly. It was almost two hours since Diana had walked away from him, and he had yet to fall asleep.

Mac punched the pillow beneath his head, then stretched, trying to take the knots out of his tense muscles. He felt the weight of the blanket over his naked body and ached for Diana. But she was scared of a man-woman relationship, he'd read that right enough.

He closed his eyes, listening to the creaky sounds of the house. She wouldn't hurt him, not knowingly. He didn't want the tenderness she evoked, the vulnerable exposure of his heart. But his feelings for Diana were just like the snow buttercups—pushing through the cold and blooming despite the forbidding elements. He ran his fingers through the hair covering his chest, remembering the touch of Diana's slender, trembling hands.

The floor boards outside his bedroom creaked slightly, and his door swung open gently. Mac eased higher on his pillow, leaning against the headboard. "Come in, Red. I can't sleep, either."

"You put Red out in the barn," Diana answered, her voice trembling. It flowed across the darkened room to shatter his tenuous peace into oblivion. "You said he gets restless this time of year—because of his ancestry."

He watched, spellbound, as Diana moved hesitantly toward him into a small patch of moonlight coming from the window. "Can't you sleep?" His voice sounded strangled, foreign to his ears.

Diana's hands tightened on her heavy robe as she shook her head. "I have to know, Mac. And I'm afraid—"

Mac's chest ached. His heart throbbed heavily as he watched her move stiffly to the edge of his bed. Studying his face, she slipped her hand into his. Her other hand tugged apart the robe, then placed his hand over her softness. "I have to know," she repeated, her tone raw with aching.

Mac knew she needed him then and fell helplessly before his own needs.

The robe slipped from her shoulders, exposing her flesh. Mac forced a swallow down his dry throat as his gaze flowed over her small shoulders, the large span of his hand on one delicate breast, then down to the gentle curves of her waist and stomach. He breathed heavily, fighting the rising urgency within him. He traced the fragile bones of her ribs and caressed her rounded hips. He had to reassure her, to say the words she needed to hear. Would he fail?

But he found there were no adequate words. Taking care, he shifted, making room for her slender body. She lifted his blankets and slipped in beside him.

For a moment he held his breath. Her body molded to his. She touched his chest, and he forced himself to relax. Her fingers stoked his corded shoulders before running through the hair on his chest.

Her breath fanned his chest as she kissed him there. "Mac?"

"Mmm?" His voice was raw with yearning. She lay her head upon his shoulder, and he could feel the very softness of her right down to his bones. He was afraid to touch her, afraid to unleash his passion. She needed time and tender caring.

Diana's thigh brushed his, and he tensed, restraining himself.

Diana breathed in Mac's masculine scent. She'd needed to know that as a woman she could satisfy a man. Now, she realized, she wanted to satisfy not just any man but only Mac. She needed Mac. To taste and enjoy. But there was more than just sensual pleasure to how she felt about him. She actually, really enjoyed being with him.

Her palm swept over his flat stomach, and she felt the quick intake of his breath. She'd never seduced a man and hadn't been sure how to go about it. She'd been bone-marrow nervous earlier. But Mac, lying willingly beneath her touch, made it so simple for her to play Cleopatra. She giggled at the thought: shy

Diana, playing the wanton; meek Diana, playing the huntress.

"What's so funny?" Mac asked, kissing her temple.

"I've just realized that I've never done this before."

"You haven't done anything yet." There was just that touch of belligerence that she liked about Mac.

"I'm going to seduce you, Mac. What do you think about that?"

He hesitated, then carefully turned her in his arms until they lay breast to chest, thigh to thigh. "Then you should get serious," he agreed with solemn dignity.

She nuzzled his nose, slipping her arms around him. Mac felt so right, she thought as he claimed her mouth in a gentle kiss. When she parted her lips, the tip of his tongue entered her to engage her in tender play.

The old bed creaked as Mac's trembling hands caressed the length of her, cherishing her. "Oh, sweetheart," he exclaimed rawly when she accepted him into her waiting body. He stilled, and she savored the feeling of him inside her. Then began the taking and the giving, the sweet passion she had yearned for.

Beneath Mac, flowing with him, seeking his mouth for a drugging kiss, Diana felt the first ripple of ecstasy and gasped.

She breathed rapidly, aware that Mac had stopped and was watching her with a frown. "Did I hurt you?"

"I feel wonderful," she whispered against his lips. She closed her eyes, feeling Mac down the length of her body, feeling his weight rest lightly upon her. She ran her hands across his shoulders, savoring his intensity, tracing the muscles beneath his heated skin.

Mac groaned when her roaming hands slid over his taut buttocks. Her hips moved restlessly. "You'd better stop that," he threatened lightly.

For the first time in her adult life, Diana felt utterly free. Against his lips, she challenged, "Make me, big guy."

Mac's mouth devoured hers. And then there was no stopping as the throbbing heat drove them on. The final burst of passion came, leaving her surprised in its wake.

Mac breathed heavily, resting upon her, his heart racing. Diana moved beneath him, treasuring Mac's utter vulnerability. Rubbing his bulky calf with her insole, she delighted in his hair-roughened texture, so different from her own.

When she caressed his shoulders, his lips parted and prowled along her throat. His unsteady breath swept across the dampened flesh over her collarbones. "You purr," he whispered against her skin as his hands lowered to stroke her breasts. "Deep little sounds that drive me crazy. I hadn't intended to let you have your way with me so quickly."

Mac shifted, keeping her breast in his palm. His fingers teased her delicate softness into a sensitive bud. Lowering his head, he kissed the satin flesh of her neck, trailing down to her breasts. "You make me hungry," he said, flicking his tongue over her aching nipples.

It was his initiation, he realized clearly. The bonding of their flesh and emotions.

Diana's body arched, and she accepted his growing passion within her. "Mac?"

"I want you," he said. "You smell so sweet, like newly cut hay. Like meadow flowers."

All softness and hungry eyes waiting, she trembled beneath him. "I could get used to a diet of you, woman. You just could be habit-forming."

Diana shifted for more space on the bed, the immovable object at her back making huge growling noises. Like a grizzly bear. Like a sawmill. She turned to look at the noisemaker. It was Mac snoring.

She tried to untangle her legs from his, but his arm looped out to hold her nearer. She rested in his light grasp, feeling the slow beat of his heart beneath her cheek.

Mac the gentle man. She nuzzled his warm hairy chest, luxuriating in the male scent. She smiled softly. There was nothing like being in Mac's arms.

"I suppose you're pretty pleased with yourself," he rumbled against her ear, his hand caressing the smoothness of her bottom. He kissed her mouth. "'Morning."

"'Morning," she returned.

He ran his thumb across her sensitive lips, his eyes darkening. "You look all soft and drowsy, lady. Like you've been making love all night."

The tender tone in his voice caused something inside her to flutter. She could have been eighteen again, and on her first date.

Mac's lips brushed hers lightly. "Nothing ever felt so much like heaven. I couldn't ask for anything sweeter than to have you in my arms."

She rubbed his cheek with her palm playfully, very much aware of their friendship changing lanes. "You're scratchy."

Mac gazed at her as though he were memorizing her face for an eternity. "You're blushing, honey," he teased, brushing the back of his hand across her cheek. "Looks good."

He'd said that as though he knew he'd caused the flush himself and was proud of it. Mac smiled slowly, his teeth shining whitely within his stubble-covered jaw. "Diana, you are a surprise," he said softly.

Her fingers trembled as they raked through his rumpled hair. She wanted him again. Wanted the raging hunger that blazed white-hot between them. And the gentleness after, the feather-soft touches and sweet murmurs that made her feel so absolutely feminine.

Mac lifted her fingers to his mouth and started suckling them, one by one. He studied her expression. "You keep looking at me like that, lady, and you'll be late for work."

Diana gasped. She traced his hard thigh, the bulky lines so different from her own.

"If...you don't stop," Mac threatened "you'll destroy all my good intentions...."

She giggled, feeling very young and very desired as she slipped from his bed. "Poor Mac."

Looking like the supremely satisfied male, Mac placed his hands behind his head and watched her slip on the worn robe. His intense gaze did nothing to calm the tempest within her.

Diana's fingers trembled as she tightened the sash around her waist. Good heavens, she'd been married and had two grown sons! How could the sight of a man—rumpled and unshaved—lying on a very disheveled bed, cause her heart to race?

She turned, feeling the tug of desire weaken her legs. Diana took a deep breath and forced herself to walk to the door.

"Nice fanny," she heard him murmur in a low, totally sexy tone. "Has a neat little sway to it."

That afternoon, Mac waited for Diana to get off work. He felt as tense as a cougar on the high mesas, while Diana had a definite cat-that-got-the-cream look. He felt that he'd given her just about as much rein as he could...especially with Terry Blakely hanging around like a mangy old wolf.

Mac leaned against a wall, cradling a cup of hot coffee in his hands as he watched Diana concentrate on the computer. Seated beneath a trophy rack of elk horns, she looked like a flower in a junk pile of cans and papers.

Dressed in a yellow turtleneck sweater and jeans, Diana glanced up and caught him staring at her. Even though a rack of fishing rods and a counter separated them, he saw the glow that lighted up her face.

Something special happened now when Diana looked at him. She was filled by a special kind of warmth that hadn't been there before their lovemaking.

The stare held and heated, and Mac gripped his cup tighter to keep from walking straight for her.

She turned away from him at last to concentrate on her work, and Mac studied the slender length of her neck rising above the yellow wool.

Diana frowned, rose and pushed a stock ladder against the shelves. She climbed up the four steps to the salmon-egg shelf and began counting the brightly colored jars.

Mac savored the neatly turned curve of her backside. Diana had gained just enough weight to enhance her curves, and her face had lost that tight pinched look of when they'd first met.

His visual appreciation stopped abruptly when he saw Blakely appraising those same feminine curves.

Sidestepping the how-to-catch-kokanee-salmon display, Mac headed for Diana. Blakely had no right to all that softness, not a bit, he decided darkly as Diana climbed down the ladder and bent to lift a heavy box.

"I'll do it," he said tightly, moving behind the counter. "It's too heavy for you, Diana."

She stared up at him, frowning. "I'm just fine, Mac. I've lifted heavier boxes."

"You'll hurt yourself," he stated, noting her darkening expression at his sharp tone. "Let Wingman or someone else do it. Or wait for me."

Diana's head tilted ever so slightly. The toe of her jogging shoe tapped the worn board flooring. "Now, Mac..." she began too softly.

"I mean it." He glared down at her, feeling as though he'd like to plant one on Blakely's amused jaw. Because he felt raw, uncertain as to her feelings or his emotions, he came down hard.

Her eyes widened. "Oh, is that an order from his royal highness?"

Blakely snickered and leaned his elbow against the counter. "Sounds like a regular brawl starting over here, Neil. Come on. The lovebirds are about to have it out."

Mac turned slowly, facing Blakely. "You stay the hell out of this, Terry."

Blakely straightened away from the counter, crossing his arms across his chest. "You've been aching to take me for years, old man. Maybe now is the time. You've got an ugly streak in you, and maybe the little woman has just discovered it. Maybe she'd like to go out once in a while and have a little fun, instead of being holed up with an old skunk like you. Is that right, Diana?"

Blakely had hit Mac's tender spot. He'd been brooding all day, wondering if he should court Diana properly. She needed more from a man than just his passionate hunger. Taking her out to the town dinner and dance tonight seemed like just the thing.

But he didn't like Blakely pointing out his rough spots. The hunting guide had chaffed his backside for years and today, Mac decided he'd had enough.

"Where's the ring, Mac?" Blakely prodded. "There's something phony about this whole deal."

Just as Mac took one threatening step toward Blakely, Diana placed a hand on his chest, stopping him. Immediately, his own rose to cover it. "Mac's flying us to Creede the first chance we have, aren't you, Mac?" she asked, her eyes sending him be-good messages.

He nodded, his eyes not leaving Blakely's. For years, he'd suspected the younger man of taking out rich hunters on illegal trophy trips. Diana wasn't a trophy, and Blakely wasn't coming near her.

"She's not like Eleanor, Mac." Blakely's eyes narrowed as the two big men gauged each other. "You can't stick her up there in that deserted house. Diana's the type who's used to socializing—"

"Mac is taking me to the town dinner and dance tonight," Diana put in smoothly. "Aren't you, honey-bear?"

Blakely's brows rose high. "Honey-bear? Old hermit Mac?" He laughed, doubling over and holding his ribs. "Tell me, what are the mating habits of a hermit?"

Mac tensed. "I don't suppose you know anything about Old Bob. Do you, Terry?" Mac asked quietly, aware that Diana had looped her arm around his waist almost protectively.

Without shifting his body or taking his eyes off Blakely's dying grin, Mac felt his insides turn into melted butter. Diana's face, full of concern, turned up at him; her wide brown eyes questioned him silently. A worried frown puckered her brows. She'd moved into his house, and now it seemed she wanted to keep him safe.

"Old Bob took a high-caliber bullet in his brisket last night. He's dead," Mac said gently, feeling her shoulder shake beneath his hand.

Diana's expressive face turned hot as he knew she would. They'd both been too wrapped in their love-making to hear a rifle shot just a few yards from the house.

"What happens now?" she asked.

"Could have been a warning," Blakely said, his expression bland. "You've been upsetting people with that chopper flying at all hours of the night."

"Could have been a warning," Mac repeated, smoothing Diana's tense shoulders. He didn't want her to have any part of the ugliness that was poaching. "The sheriff made plaster casts of footprints I'd found by that stand of aspen trees just off the meadow. He's got a few clues."

He kissed Diana's soft lips lightly, savoring the taste of her. He needed her alone and away from Blakely's narrowed eyes.

"Let's go home," she whispered, easing from him to turn off the computer. "I want to bake a pie for the dance."

"I'll be there, Diana," Blakely stated, watching her. "See you later."

Mac felt the emptiness where Diana had stood with her arms around him. Could he let her go when she decided it was time for her to leave?

The hell with letting her go.

That evening, Diana glanced at Mac's profile, at the taut jaw and furrowed brow. In the light of the pick-up's dashboard, she could see his smooth-shaved jaw slide, as though he were gritting his teeth. Despite his black mood, he looked . . . quite handsome.

Mac's groomed attire contrasted with the older man's, seated on the other side of Diana. Clancy exuded the flavor of a rough cowboy down to his boots and his chewing tobacco.

Diana's gaze drifted back to Mac. His carefully combed hair just touched the collar of his gray West-ern-style suit. The cut emphasized his broad shoulders, and his woodsy after-shave added to his country-boy image. He turned, his gaze warming as it strolled down her formfitting green sweater-dress. Her breasts tingled as his stare lingered there. He was remembering, she knew, aware that his hand had moved to cup her knee. His thumb rubbed the inside of her leg slowly.

"You know, when I said, 'Let's skip the doings and have a night out at Creede,' I didn't mean bring Clancy along, too," he whispered.

"Shh." She nudged him with her shoulder. "He just wanted a ride."

Mac scowled at the craggy musher, who seemed oblivious to their conversation, though he sat next to Diana. "We're stuck with him. My plans didn't call for a threesome."

Diana placed her hand over his on the steering wheel—she loved touching Mac—feeling just a twinge of remorse. When Clancy had asked for a ride, she'd actually been relieved. She'd felt as nervous about tonight as though it were her first date, and she knew Clancy's presence would ease the tension.

She was right. Clancy had an absolutely marvelous time at Howard's Cantina, noisily devouring a full rack of barbecued ribs and preventing intimate conversation. As Mac glowered at him for an ill-disguised burp, Clancy sat back to blow the suds off his beer. "Hey, why don't you two kids cut a rug? The music sounds good. May dance with Diana myself, later maybe, after a few more brews. Reminds me of good times up the Yukon, mushing. We'd sit around, enjoy the company of a good woman. There was a woman up there who could warm your—"

"Oh, hell, Clancy, you've never been up the Yukon," Mac said in a tone that reminded Diana of Red's low growl.

"Sure was, entered dogsledding races all the time. But it was awful cold in the winter. Ran a lot of dogs in my time, though. Been meaning to ask you if I could use Red to break in a new team of sled dogs. Think I could borrow him?"

Mac leaned back in his chair, contemplating the old-timer darkly. His long dark fingers laced with Diana's slender ones, his thumb stroking her palm. "Clancy, if you'll manage to lose yourself for a few hours, I'll let you borrow Red."

The older man grinned widely and rose. "Okay by me. Thought my plan would work. Sorry about Old Bob, Mac. Call for me over at Charlie's back room just before you decide to light out. They got a good poker game going, I hear."

Then bending gallantly, he took Diana's hand and kissed the back of it before walking off.

"Blackmail," Mac accused, muttering as Clancy wove between the restaurant's round tables. "That old man can be a real nuisance. He's not teaching you dog-pushing. It's too dangerous."

Diana fought the smile playing about her mouth. Since the evening was so special, she decided not to tell Mac that she had already had her first run. Clancy had even praised her.

The country quartet played a two-step, and Mac grinned at her. "Want to try out the floor?"

He had such an expectant air about him that she couldn't bear to start an argument. Freed from Clancy, Mac was all smiles and sexy promising looks.

Once on the dance floor, Mac wrapped his arms around her waist. She leaned back, startled by the un-conventional stance. "People dance like this now, honey. Trust me," he said.

They danced slowly, barely swaying with the music as his strong thighs moved against hers. With her head tucked beneath his chin and her cheek resting over his slow-beating heart, she let herself imagine they were in love.

There it was again, she thought. That feeling of being feminine and desirable, as though she were with her first beau. The years didn't exist when Mac held her close, and she let her barriers slip a little more.

Mac nuzzled her temple, kissing it. "You're aw-fully quiet, Diana."

When she leaned back to look up at him, Mac's tender gaze changed into a dark smoldering look. Re-minded of how devastatingly attractive Mac had looked that morning—stretched out on the rumpled bed, his hair disheveled by her fingers—Diana closed her eyes and snuggled to Mac's warm secure chest.

Swaying in his arms, Diana lost herself to the music and Mac. He just felt so...right. She looked up and studied the endearing familiar lines of his face. How could a man's mouth be so firm and yet so tender?

While staring at the sensuous line, Diana felt rip-ples of excitement coursing through her body. The hot ripples of excitement that belonged to a young woman with her first love. "Oh, Mac," she whispered help-lessly, confused by her emotions.

"'Oh, Mac,'" he repeated teasingly. "I like that—you gasping my name with that sexy little tone." He moved her into a dark corner of the room, his tall body hiding her from others. He watched her waiting expression intently, then raised his hand to her face. He touched her eyebrows, then trailed his fingers down to her cheeks.

His touch was so like him—gentle with a raspy texture that excited. His thumb stroked her bottom lip, and his gaze darkened. His breath was coming more quickly. His face was all intense, as if nothing else mattered but this moment in time. Then Mac lowered his head, taking her mouth.

He rubbed his lips across her parted ones, savoring their softness. With a slight movement of her head, she rested her cheek against his palm.

Framing her small face within his hand, Mac barely breathed. When the tip of her tongue slid over his lips, then dipped inside, he trembled. In her warm moistness, he tasted the heady desire of a woman.

Placing his forehead against hers, Mac whispered, "It's been a long day."

She rubbed his nose with hers. "Has it? Shall we go home?" She saw the excitement in his eyes.

"We've still got to pick up that damned Clancy," he said.

Mac paid their bill, then eased her into her winter coat. He adjusted the collar carefully, then kept his arm around her as they walked into the night. Diana leaned against him, savoring the hard strength of his lean body. He held her to him, as though she were a necessary part of him, of his life.

She felt a tiny ripple of uneasiness. Mac's lovemaking took her to the heights, but he had a tendency to want his own way, which sometimes rankled her. This darker side of his passion intrigued her, too. She just had to prod it a little, explore. . . .

She also wanted to flirt outrageously with him. The thought shocked her at first, then enticed her.

Passing through the darkened alley to the pickup, Diana couldn't resist putting her arm around his waist, then slipping it lower until it reached Mac's firm buttocks. After all, he'd surprised her once or twice.

He paused, glancing down at her. "You're playing with fire," he murmured in a provocative tone that sent excitement down to her toes. "You'd better keep your distance."

For a moment Diana hesitated, waylaid by the novelty of the situation—forty-two was an odd time to start feeling her sensual oats. But Mac had this aura about him of masterful self-control that just begged for a mussing. Feeling the challenge course through her, Diana stopped to lock her arms around him. She was surprised to hear herself asking, "What if I don't want to?"

She could feel him tense, as though he was struggling to keep piercing emotions leashed. Something within her wanted to lift the lid to those feelings, to taste the raw male desire he tempered so well.

Deliberately she stood on tiptoe to trace the line of his mouth with the tip of her tongue. Just to give her that special edge, she tugged his face nearer to blow in his ear.

When Mac went taut as his bow strings, Diana felt a jolt of sheer feminine satisfaction. She just had to taste the tempting whorl of his ear with her tongue.

"Now you've done it." Mac gathered her to him like a man who had waited years for the taste of her. Diana trembled, fighting the demanding ache within her, then yielded to her immediate need to touch Mac.

As she eased his coat open, he groaned and said, "Unbutton my shirt, let me feel you touch me."

His trembling hands pulled her sweater up as her fingers fumbled at exposing his enticing chest.

"You aren't wearing a bra, lady," he exclaimed, staring at the hardened tips of her breasts. He was breathing hard, his eyes widened in shock. "You mean every man in there could have brushed against you, danced with you and felt this?"

Just this once Diana forgave him for dishing out his macho talk. Teasing Mac was absolutely delightful. Pressing her breasts against his bare chest, she grinned up at him. In this mood, he made her feel as though life were just beginning. "But Mac, isn't this nice?"

"Mmm, nice. I could make a meal of you," he whispered huskily, his fingers caressing her.

She kissed the hard line of his lips, softened by previous kisses. "I like your mouth on me," she admitted shyly, watching his eyes darken and the deep red color flag his cheeks. She watched his reaction, knowing that this was the very first time she had encouraged a man's blatant hunger. Mac didn't need encouragement as he lifted her on tiptoe for a soul-shattering kiss.

"You don't know what you do to me," he admitted unevenly.

Diana's ego soared outrageously, and she couldn't resist a pleased smile.

"You'd better worry about your effect on me, woman," he continued, a sensuous smile lurking around his mouth. "I can't take much more. I feel like I'm a kid making out in the back seat."

She traced the enticing curve of his lips. "Mac, don't you think we're...a little old for making out in dimly lit alleys?"

"A man can only stand so much temptation, woman. I hadn't counted on this, either. Somehow, when you get near me, all my good intentions are blown to smithereens."

For his ego-bolstering admission, Diana decided to give Mac the most seductive kiss she could ever hope to give in her life. When she was finished, she nibbled on his lobe, enjoying the unsteady way he breathed. She smiled, nuzzling against his throat. "Don't fight me. I intend to have my way with you again."

"Diana." He gasped as her tongue gently traced his ear. "There's more to this than... I mean, we're friends, aren't we? I wouldn't take advantage of the situation.... Hell, you deserve champagne and roses."

Diana whispered, "I know, but for now there's this...."

Seven

—

At two o'clock in the morning, after dropping Clancy off at his house, Mac let Red outside, then pulled Diana to him. "Come here, you."

Once his mouth fitted to hers, fireworks started exploding. Hungry and demanding, his body radiated a hard male need. Diana couldn't wait to touch him, to feel the steely planes of his chest. She gasped as he swung her up in his arms and started to carry her toward the bedroom.

Diana couldn't get enough of his kisses, his taste. The groans coming from deep in his throat ignited her.

When they were halfway across the living room, Red began barking, and Mac shuddered, his arms tightening around her as though he never wanted to let her go. "Someone is here," he whispered against the side of her neck. His left hand gently rubbed the small of her back. "Red's got that special bark."

He kissed her lips, the wild heat of his cheeks warming her own. Slowly, very reluctantly, Mac lowered her to her feet. "Don't move one step."

When Mac finally released her, Diana wondered if her knees could support her. She closed her eyes, listening to the sound of his voice outside. She wanted to hear him whisper those sweet things to her in the blackness of the night. Impatient to have him against her, she gripped a pillow from the couch and hugged it to ease the aching.

Gradually, Diana realized that another man was talking to Mac. She listened intently. The man's voice was familiar. Mac swung the door open, and beneath the harsh light of the porch light, she saw Blaine.

Diana's eyes locked with her son's. She hadn't seen him in weeks, and now Blaine's young face looked weary.

"Come in," Mac invited the younger man, his eyes catching Diana's.

Blaine stepped inside the room, watching her almost warily. A younger image of his father, Blaine looked around the cozy room bearing Diana's neat touch.

She wanted to run to him and embrace him, but Blaine's accusing stare rooted her to the spot and caused her to lock her fingers tighter around the pillow.

"Hello, Mother. I've been waiting for you to come home," he said with Alex's you've-done-it-this-time tone.

"Hello, Blaine," she managed to say calmly. But she really wanted to say, "I'm glad to see you—I love you. But why are you here now and like this?"

Mac moved quietly to her side. She found his warmth and substance reassuring. "You're welcome to stay here, Blaine," he said.

Remembering her manners, Diana introduced Mac. "Blaine, this is—" *My host? My lover?* "—Mac," she finished quietly.

Blaine stared at Mac. "You're nothing like Dad. You're exactly what I wouldn't think my mother would pick for a mid-life affair." The statement bore the stamp of Alex's elegant distaste.

Mac's head tilted a little, as though he'd just received a very small jab. "Blaine, that's enough," Diana said, plumping the pillow to still her shaking hands. Fighting layers of self-doubt, Diana faced her son's silent accusations. "Mac is—"

"You don't have to say anything, Diana." Mac crossed his arms over his chest. "You're welcome to stay, Blaine. But you will not insult your mother."

Blaine turned to Diana. "I know who he is—your boyfriend. He broke up you and Dad. Dad told me so. I just had to see it for myself. I didn't believe it, but now I know it's true."

Diana tossed the pillow to the couch. Her sons had never seen the full extent of her temper; she really did not intend to lose control now. "What did you say?" she asked carefully.

"Rick said it couldn't be true. That whatever was happening came after the divorce."

"That's enough, son," Mac said quietly.

Lifting her hand to silence Mac, Diana felt a cold chill sweeping across her flesh. Holding Blaine's eyes, she said, "It's all right, Mac. I wasn't unfaithful to your father, Blaine." She wanted to lace her fingers with Mac's, to use his strength.

Her sons' love was the cornerstone of her life; she had to fight to keep Rick and Blaine from slipping farther and farther away from her. But she needed time to think, and Blaine needed time to calm down and get some rest. "Why don't you get some sleep, and we'll talk in the morning."

Blaine glanced around the room. "I've seen all I need to see. I'm taking off tonight—"

"There's plenty of room, Blaine," Mac interrupted, his dark eyes flowing over Diana's taut face.

"Let me handle this, Mac," she ordered quietly, facing her son fully. "You're staying the night, Blaine."

His rebellious stare locked with hers. Diana returned it evenly. "It's a nice bed," she added, watching his indecision. "Why don't you stay the whole weekend?"

"I drove nonstop from Missouri just to see you. I took off right after my last class." Blaine stated haughtily, glaring at Mac.

"Oh, shut up," Diana said as coolly as she could manage. Somewhere, somehow, her son had acquired an arrogance that grated on her nerves. She wondered briefly about the lovable little boy she had kissed good-night. "So help me, Blaine. Your manners are inexcusable. You always were something of a pain—"

Blaine stepped back, shock written on his face. "Mother!"

Diana thought she heard Mac chuckle, but when she turned blazing eyes to him, his face was positively too innocent. "You shut up, too."

"Yes, ma'am," Mac murmured contritely.

She glared up at him and then at Blaine. Men, the both of them. Men, with their possessiveness. The indignant son and the overprotective...friend. "Go get your things, Blaine. Mac can make a bed, and he'll show you where to sleep. I'm going to bed now, and I don't want to hear any...angry noises in the night. Or you can leave."

"Mother!"

Diana firmly turned her back and walked into her room. She closed the door with a soft but final click.

She paused, then jerked open the door. Her son stood uncertainly in the center of the room. "Blaine, Mac was not the cause of the divorce. And while you're in this house, you show some good manners."

She closed the door to lean back against it, shaking.

Diana watched the leafless branches sway in the winter wind, the silvery moon hiding behind a passing cloud. She tried to force the tension from her as she sat in the ancient cherry rocker.

Mac shouldn't have to put up with all of this, she thought. He deserved better than a woman's coming-out experience and an enraged son standing on his doorstep.

Diana pressed her hands against her thighs, hating the uncertainty. She knew her body's needs, felt the melting hot heat build in her. She massaged her temples, hoping to ease the ache. Lying in bed with Mac, she'd felt consumed...and it frightened her. "I'm old enough to be a grandmother," she whispered shakily.

She didn't want to care again at her age. She hadn't planned on Mac. But she had practically thrown herself into his arms. Mac was just too potent.

She wrapped her robe tighter around her, acknowledging the sensual tightness in her body. She wanted Mac. Wanted his hands on her, wanted his lips on hers, wanted the rough-tender way he touched her, as though she were his alone and he really cared. She shivered, fighting for control. Sex wasn't love, and she'd already had her chance.

Did love come courting a second time around? Or was Mac just part of her mid-life crisis?

Game time was over, she decided. She wanted to start thinking of Mac in terms longer than a few days. He'd become her necessary edge—the tender man. A man to endure the hardships and a man to stir up the excitement in her. She could trust him until the end of time, and that was worth fighting for. She cared for him, and it was time to define the terms of their relationship.

One fact stared her in the face—she had to come to terms with her son. For years she'd compromised her essence to her family. She'd played the generic mother who never regretted a moment.... She intended to stand on her own finally. She'd explain it all to Blaine and make sure he understood. She couldn't lose his love.

Diana's lids fluttered and she realized she was finally falling asleep. But she had barely nodded off when she became aware of Mac's woodsy scent. He was lifting her from the chair. "Come on, sleepy head," he said, "it's bed for you. We'll take care of all your problems tomorrow."

For the first time since childhood, Diana was tucked in and kissed good-night.

Sleepy, she encircled his neck with her arms and held him tight against her. She wanted Mac. The snuggly craggy warm feel of him next to her. "Hold me."

He chuckled, brushing a curl back from her face. "I do that and we'll both be in trouble. Your son isn't the understanding type right now. Go to sleep."

She turned her face toward the pillow, accepting the gentle touch of his hand on her cheek. She kissed the rough palm lightly. "You are really a nice man."

"Uh-huh. But it's costing me plenty, honey. I probably won't sleep a wink."

Diana had to tell him. "I never thanked you for taking me out tonight. I'd thought I was too old to start needing again."

Mac's big hand trembled as he caressed her forehead. "The last I heard, there were no age barriers on needing, honey. Nothing could be righter than what's between us."

He could always go back to playing bagpipes at midnight, Mac decided grimly, watching Diana's slender form shift beneath her robe as she cooked breakfast. When she turned to him, holding the platters of bacon and eggs, Mac knew he'd remember her forever.

A man doesn't easily forget a sleepy-eyed woman with tousled sunlit hair and sweet, sweet lips. When Diana made love to him, she forced out his loneliness, replacing it with her fire.

Blaine had come to claim his mother, and Mac fought the sour taste of losing Diana. Somehow, the trick on Benevolence had backfired.

She placed the eggs and bacon on the table, her teeth nibbling at her bottom lip as she checked the table settings for the third time. "Who called this morning, Mac? I heard the phone ring."

Mac scowled, avoiding her searching look. "Something about Old Bob's death. The sheriff found the same high-caliber rifle casings near an illegal elk kill. . . . You're going back, aren't you?"

"No."

Blaine entered the kitchen, stopping just inside the doorway. "Of course, she is."

Diana turned slowly to face her son. Mac noted the trembling of her hands, the tightening of her fingers on the salt and pepper shakers. "We need to talk about that, Blaine. Would you like to walk with me after breakfast?"

Mac felt the fear grow in him, felt it wrap tight around his heart. His life spread before him like an empty void, Diana's warmth already fading. . . .

Why did he have to open his heart to her?

Wasn't losing one woman enough pain in a man's lifetime?

The noon wind was cold, tossing her hair against her face. Diana glanced at the stark mountains topped with snow and said quietly, "I like it here, Blaine. There's the peace I've needed for a long time."

Her son placed his hand against the barn, prodding a rock with his toe. "I can see something between you and Mac. You have a sort of glow now.... Do you really care for him, Mom?" he asked slowly.

"Yes, I do." She caressed his cheek, realizing how much he had gone through. "I love you and Rick, but there's another side of me, too. Mac is the gentlest man I know. He's made me happy. You want that, don't you?"

Blaine cleared his throat, frowning. "It's over between you and Dad, then? For real?"

She ruffled his hair as she had when he was small. Smiling gently, she answered, "It was over a long time ago. Meeting Mac, staying here, was an accident. But I'm so very glad he happened in my life, Blaine. I hope you'll understand."

Her son stared down at her for a long time before he took her hand. "I was pretty mean last night, wasn't I?"

Smiling, she hugged him. "Pretty awful. Come back to me, honey."

"I love you, Mom," he said simply, returning the hug. "Rick said you were out on a 'voyage of self-discovery.' He said to give you space. I should have had more faith—"

"Shh. You're here now and you understand. That's what counts."

"Blaine has talked with his father about Thanksgiving, Mac. Alex has already made plans, so Blaine is going to spend Thanksgiving with us. Is that all right?'' Diana asked that evening after supper. Seated on the couch, Diana acted like the perfect hostess.

Mac fought his visions of loneliness, hiding behind the barricade of the local newspaper. He could feel panic rippling up his spine. He'd almost kept her, but now her son had arrived to claim her. Why hadn't he put his courting plans in high gear?

Mac could feel his teeth grind. A man couldn't bank on seduction, not when he wanted a woman like Diana to stay put.

Over the top of his newspaper, he glanced at her stealthily. Dressed in jeans and a bulky maroon sweater, she looked so beautiful. Mac shifted uncomfortably in his worn armchair, rereading the ''Game Warden's Column'' for the third time. He hadn't ever pulled out the stops when it came to wooing her, and the idea nettled him. He'd never played the part of a Romeo yet, but to keep Diana from leaving him and returning to that no-good ex-husband of hers, he just might. . . .

''Mac, are you sleeping?'' Diana asked, leaning forward to tug his paper lower. ''I asked if Blaine could share Thanksgiving with us.''

Mac allowed himself to drown in her brown velvet gaze, allowed it to sweep inside him, warming. He grinned slowly, watching the soft curve of her mouth return the gesture. ''I'd really like that, Diana. In fact, why don't you invite Rick, too?''

''Really? You wouldn't mind having a houseful? Rick has a girlfriend who would die of loneliness if they were separated.''

Blaine shifted, reaching down to pet Red's shaggy head. "Ah, Mom, I haven't had time to tell you about my girlfriend, Cindy. She's ... ah ..."

"She can come, too. This is lovely! A whole houseful of kids for the holidays, Mac. Isn't it great?" Diana clapped her hands, bouncing off the couch. She snatched Mac's head between her hands and gave him a short kiss on the lips. "Oh, thank you, Mac."

Both males stared, fascinated as she ran to a cabinet to extract a notepad and pen.

Dazed by the sudden happy flush washing Diana's cheeks, Mac murmured, "Fine. I'd like that."

Her son took a moment to recover, his expression thoughtful before it changed to excitement. "This is great!"

Uncertain whether either person would hear him, Mac offered quietly, "It's early in the season, but if they like to ski, there's a lift not far from here. I can borrow a couple of snowmobiles, too. There's already snow in the high country on the designated trails."

Both mother and son turned to Mac, watching him intently. Mac forced a swallow as Diana's small face softened and almost glowed. They gazed at each other. "Thank you so much, Mac," she murmured huskily, lowering her lashes over tear-bright eyes.

"It's nothing, honey," he returned in as deep and intimate a tone. Fascinated by the thick damp lashes, Mac reached out a finger to dry them. "Don't cry."

Diana's mouth trembled, her hand sliding into her son's larger one. "I'm just happy, Mac."

Blaine's astute eyes shifted from his mother to Mac, meeting the older man's mild stare. "She's the weepy sort. She's cried enough sad tears, maybe the happy ones will wash them away, huh?'' he asked awkwardly, placing his arm around Diana's shoulders.

"Stop talking about me as though I weren't here, Blaine,'' Diana chided, sniffing delicately.

"Yes, Mother,'' Blaine answered too placidly, his gaze locking with Mac's quiet one. *Take it easy with her,* his stare warned. *Don't hurt her.*

Slowly, Mac extended his hand to the younger man, who gripped it. "I imagine we'd both better help your mother, before she spins herself into exhaustion, don't you think, Blaine?''

"Agreed.''

Diana sniffed again and wiped her eyes. "Mac, I won't have you talking around me, either.''

Watching her, Mac spoke to Blaine, "She's a soft one.''

"And men talk about women chattering,'' Diana teased, her eyes sparkling. "Let's get busy!''

Thanksgiving arrived in a flurry of giggling girlfriends, happy sons, a beaming Mac and the scents of a roast turkey dinner. A layer of new snow blanketed the fields and weighted the tree branches. The sun decorated the landscape with a silvery glitter, which demanded a pre-Thanksgiving dinner snowball fight between the younger couples.

Diana couldn't resist drawing Mac into a corner of the porch. She grinned as he angled his tall body away from the threatening heap of skis. Hugging him tightly around his lean waist, she pressed her cheek to his chest. She nuzzled his well-washed sweatshirt with her cold nose. "This is so nice of you, Mac.''

Mac glanced uncomfortably at the foursome fast approaching from the meadow.

"You can hug me too, you know," she offered happily. "Oh, Mac, I'm so happy. I feel like those kids—bursting with life, ready to meet new challenges. What's wrong?" she asked, looking up into his wary face.

"Look behind you."

Diana turned slowly, her arms still wrapped around Mac's waist. Watching her with unreadable faces were Rick and Blaine, snowballs poised in their gloves. The two girls looked anxiously from the brothers to Diana.

She turned to look at Mac's flushed face and grinned. "Are you embarrassed?" she asked, releasing him. "You'll have to hold your own with them, big guy. They have some idea you're after their mother."

Even during dinner, Diana couldn't resist teasing Mac. She kept shooting him intimate glances over the food-laden table, just to torment him a little. He was so cute in his new cream-colored sweater, stammering now and then and appearing to wait for the ax to fall.

Just as Mac reached for his second helping of pumpkin pie, Diana couldn't resist saying, "I have a little secret, guys. Want to share it?"

Blaine's filled mouth stopped chewing. Rick's fork stopped midway to his lips.

Struggling to keep his voice level, Rick said, "Sure, Mom. What gives?"

Diana glanced at Mac, who looked as though he'd like to be dangling from a hundred-foot ski lift or rappelling down a rock cliff—anywhere but seated with her family. When Mac silently pleaded with her,

Diana couldn't resist licking the dollop of whipped cream from her fork.

The come-hither gesture almost caused Mac to break out in a sweat. Just for extra spice, Diana trailed her fingertip across the back of his hand. To her delight, Mac's cheeks began to flush. "Mac and I have been playing a little joke on Benevolence."

"How so?" Blaine asked cautiously, alert to Mac's uncomfortable expression.

"To win a championship chili contest, Mac announced our engagement." Diana winked at Mac. "It's called 'influencing the judge.' Isn't that right?"

"Mother!" Both Rick and Blaine looked as though they would go into permanent shock. Cindy and Alise giggled, as usual, and Diana found herself joining them. She laughed until the tears began to roll down her cheeks.

Rick recovered enough to say, "Mother, this isn't funny."

"Why not? I think it's hilarious."

Blaine emitted a noise that sounded suspiciously like a chuckle. "A whole town, Mom?"

"And surrounding homesteads. I rather like putting Mac on the spot, too."

Rick's expression began to shift, a grin toying with his mouth. "Having fun, Mom?"

"For the first time in eons. I really don't have a care in the world." Diana felt as though she'd shot through the walls of her box. The one that had kept her prisoner for so many years. The right and proper box that stripped her essence and demanded her soul.

Blaine lifted his water glass in a toast. "Here's to Mom. You deserve a little fun."

Diana looked at Mac's oh-my-gosh expression. "And now to cap off our first new-family holiday, Mac will play the bagpipes."

Later, when Mac decided to carry in the firewood for the night, both younger men donned their coats to follow him.

There, behind the house, standing before the woodpile, Rick and Blaine faced Mac. The light snow drifted between them, covering their shoulders. "It's time to talk," Rick announced.

Blaine adjusted his knit cap and raised his collar higher against the winter wind. "Mom's having fun. Even an idiot could see how happy she is."

"Mom hasn't laughed like that for a long time. Especially when you offered to dance the Highland fling," Rick added.

"She did like showing me up when she did her own dance," Mac agreed, wondering why in Sam Hill he felt as though he was being interviewed.

Blaine propped a boot on a snow-covered log. "Mom even likes her job. I didn't know she knew anything about fishing or hunting. Seems like she knows some interesting hunting guides, too. She's stopped acting...so strained. It's like she's a kid again."

Both youths looked at Mac expectantly.

"If this little talk is going to take long, I vote we adjourn to the tack room in the barn," he offered warily.

Rick stood up, dusting the snow from him. "Suits me. Let's go."

The tack room was warm, scented of hay and animals and old leather. Mac lighted the kerosene lantern and fired the small potbellied stove. Rick carefully adjusted his length to a rickety wooden box. Blaine looked around, then settled into a chair next to a table. He shuffled the worn deck of cards he pulled out of his coat pocket. "Poker?"

"Count me in." Rick watched Mac. "How about you?"

On the third hand of stud poker, Rick leaned back on the wooden box. He shuffled the cards slowly. "What gives with you, Mac? Just what are your intentions toward Mom?"

"She's been hurt enough," Blaine asserted. "We understand now that Dad has a lot to answer for. We just got mixed up, somehow. It wasn't hard to do, considering the way she kept everything inside while Dad kept laying blame." He paused. "So what gives between you and her?"

Being interviewed by a woman's sons was a novel experience, Mac decided quickly. How could he say that he needed her like air?

Before he could answer, Blaine continued. "She likes this new independence thing. I think she should be encouraged to do what she wants. She deserves it, don't you think, Mac?"

"And what about this marriage thing, Mac?" Rick asked, frowning. "Just what are your intentions there? After all, a guy likes to think his mother is sacred, you know?"

"I want Diana to be happy," Mac answered with all the strength of his convictions.

Blaine toyed with a saddle buckle. "Oh, she's happy. We can see that. But what are you intending in the long run? I mean, the town is bound to get wise to the joke someday. You wouldn't leave her holding the bag, would you?''

''Diana will have to decide how to handle the matter. She's making her own decisions. For my part, I care deeply for her. If she stayed, I couldn't ask for much more out of life.'' Mac retrieved a bottle of red wine from beneath an Apache saddle blanket.

''You're not a boozer, are you?'' Rick asked sharply, looking at the half-filled bottle. ''Just how much do you drink?''

''Oh, lay off, Rick,'' Blaine interrupted. ''The guy must be all of—'' he looked at Mac appraisingly ''—well, he's got a few years on him, but he seems to be in pretty good shape... for his age. If he drank heavily, we'd know it by now.''

Mac couldn't resist grinning as he poured the wine into three tin cups. ''Thanks. We old-timers need all the help we can get.''

Holding his drink, Rick looked around the small room. ''I suppose you own all this. I mean, Mom isn't going to get into any financial trouble here, is she?''

Rick shrugged. ''It's over now. But somehow, Mom just didn't come up even when she and Dad split. There was no compensation for all that time she spent at home. It took a while for her to get on her feet, I guess. I remember looking at her one day and thinking, 'Mom looks like she's breaking in two.'''

Mac frowned, realizing how Diana had passed through so many difficult trials. No wonder she looked like a stray when she arrived on his doorstep. Why couldn't life have brought them together sooner? Why had she suffered alone? ''I'm financially stable. She won't be responsible for any debts.''

Rick nodded. "That's good. Now, ah, Mom is pretty, ah, righteous about marriage. I mean—" He swallowed a sip and glanced nervously at Blaine, then back at Mac. "She likes to tease you, like a girl, almost. And she touches you, like guys our age." He took a deep breath. "What I mean to say is, we don't want you taking advantage of her . . . innocence about the world. Do you have any problems with that?"

Mac met Rick's probing stare evenly. Diana had come to him, offering herself so sweetly to him. "Your mother and I are friends. I wouldn't do anything to hurt her."

Blaine pondered Mac's statement a moment. "I like that, Rick. Basically, I think the guy is okay."

"What about a real marriage?" Rick persisted. "There are lots of guys our ages turning up with baby brothers and sisters."

Mac closed his eyes. Making a child with Diana would be the sweetest thing in the world. But if he couldn't have that, he'd settle for any scrap of Diana possible. "I'd vote for marriage in a minute. I intend to try my damnedest to keep her any way I can."

"Whatever is happening is good for Mom. She's put on some pounds, and she's looking great. . . . Here's to her new life." Rick lifted the bottle.

The door squeaked open. "Here's to snowballs!" Diana yelled, pitching her snowball straight at Mac. It struck his cheek before he could duck.

"Here's to bull sessions!" Cindy lofted her missile straight toward Blaine while Alise plastered Rick's face.

"Women! You can't trust 'em," Blaine crowed, reforming the snow sliding down his face and running after the escaping females. "We'll teach you. Bull sessions are sacred to the American male!"

Mac slowly wiped his cheek, feeling his grin spread through him. "I believe Humpty can be put back together again. Once the house is quiet, she won't stand a chance. I am going to keep that woman. The question is how."

Eight

The huskies easily pulled Clancy's light sled over the powdery dry snow. Standing on the sled's back runners, her stomach braced against the seat, Diana finally felt as free as the golden eagle soaring through the sunlit morning.

With a fantastic Thanksgiving and Christmas behind her—her sons had obviously enjoyed spending their holiday vacations at Mac's—Diana expected the whole new year to follow suit. January was the perfect time to begin anew, to braid the past into the future.

Snow glistened on the San Juan Mountains; the fields and forests were draped with the heavy white blanket. The freezing wind ruffled the fur lining of her parka hood and stung her cheeks. But dark goggles protected her eyes.

She'd borrowed the sled for her day off, wanting— no, burning—to make her private run, to explore without Mac's anxious eye or Clancy's cautions.

Red, acting as lead dog, knew the stretch well due to Clancy's frequent runs. Across the open meadows, swinging down a snow-covered lane and then to the higher country to a lone scraggy pine tree buffeted by wind and time.

The run was her baptism, her journey to freedom, wiping away the pain and insecurities. The strength was in her, growing.

Red picked up pace, and the huskies strained against the harnesses, running toward the wilderness. The snow from their feet sprayed across Diana's face, forcing her to tuck her chin deeper in the protective knit covering. She felt elated, ready to take on anything life threw at her.

Suddenly, there was a sound like that of a rifle shot. A dead tree cracked and fell near the trail.

In her mind's eye, she saw Mac. The gentle man with dark lighting eyes. He was a part of it all, the rebirth. Concentrating on him, Diana could feel the womanly essence tingle within her. She had been a girl when she'd married Alex, trusting him to form their lives. But with Mac, there was sharing.

She thought of Mac's behavior lately. Grumpy, wary, sidestepping any intimacy. She was certain that Mac watched her; she could feel him waiting. For what?

How could she let him know she wanted all of him now? How in the world did a woman pursue a man?

For just an instant, a sharp fear chilled her. She gripped the sled tighter. Mac was a born protector, a Colorado knight championing the wounded and the needy. Was she taking advantage of his tender heart?

The sled hit a hidden branch, bumping the runners beneath her boots. Diana controlled the sled, then called to Red, who had slowed his pace. "Hey, Red! Go for it!"

Go for it. It was her time. Her life was swinging in a new direction just as the sled coursed across the unmarked sunlit snow. She was a woman controlling her own destiny, finding confidence within.

But she needed Mac to complete her life.

In an alpine clearing, Diana noted Clancy's marker—a burned tree stump. She caught a sound, a chopping noise overhead, and saw the shadow of Mac's helicopter sweep across the blinding snow.

He hovered overhead, and beneath her knitted face covering, Diana smiled. "Let's go, Red," she called. "Gee!"

Leaving Clancy's trail, Diana slowed the dogs with the tug rope and brake, then leaped off the sled, running beside the team. The huskies, wanting to run, fought the slower pace, barking. Red turned his head to the pack and bared his teeth. Diana ran to him and patted his head. "Let's show him we know our stuff, boy!"

Loping beside Red, Diana ignored Mac's helicopter. She was light enough to run on top of the crust of the deep snow easily. She led the dogs in a circle, and after a few times around, they made a visible trail. Diana ran to the center of the giant circle. She threw out her arms, laughing up at Mac, then tramped on the snow, forming the eyes and mouth of a smiling face.

Mac's helicopter dipped and swayed in an answer, but when she thought he would land, the craft sailed toward the high mesas.

Frowning, she followed the helicopter into the blinding sun. "That's right, Mac. You've come just close enough, it's time to run away," she whispered, remembering how he backstepped every time she came near.

Since his lingering kiss beneath the Christmas mistletoe, Mac had acted like a man on a tight leash, and she didn't know why. But she intended to find out....

Diana walked to the dogs lying in the snow, their pink tongues hanging out. Six sets of huskies' eyes watched her as Red stood and stretched. She patted Red. "You're ready to run again, aren't you? Being free is quite a feeling—it makes you stronger, huh?"

Red licked her leather glove, his giant body taut. She smiled again, feeling very young and very certain of herself as a woman.

With a lingering glance at the helicopter, Diana began to run beside the back of the sled, waiting for the dogs to pick up pace. When they were running strong, she leaped onto the back runners to brace her body against the sled. Then she gave herself to the sheer freedom of the high country.

When Diana returned the team to Clancy late that afternoon, she had decided to call Alex at the first opportunity.

"Clancy is a fourteen-carat gold-plated idiot." Muttering to himself, Mac felt raw clear through as he opened the door to his house. Seeing Diana out in the wild, trusting a half-broken pack of running dogs with her life, was a nightmare. The new bullet hole through his helicopter windshield didn't help his nerves, either.

The lack of sleep nettled him. The sheriff had enlisted his aid to catch the elusive poachers. Between the long hours in the helicopter and the sleepless hours aching for Diana, Mac kept himself going on coffee and nerves. He wanted Diana down to his bones, but a man couldn't start courting seriously when he had pushed himself to his physical limits.

He had his sights set, but candlelight and roses took plenty of time to plan. Especially when there wasn't a French restaurant or a florist shop within miles. Mac had decided to put his strategy on hold until just the right moment. Diana deserved every ounce of magic he could muster.

He could wait . . . maybe.

Having the youngsters in the house had eased his tension, but maybe Benevolence had the last laugh. Could a hermit change his spots?

"In the middle of everything, she decides to become a full-fledged musher." He swept the snow from his boots with a broom, carefully stepping on a braided rug. He eyed Diana's small fur-lined moccasins and leggings—Eskimo mukluks—as he tugged off his snow-encrusted boots. "I should have put the copter down right there and made her hit the trail back, really laid down the law. Should have followed her every step of the way. Should have knocked Clancy into the next world when he suggested such a thing. She's not even up to one of those dogs' working weight."

Mac closed the door quietly as Red padded toward him. Taking off his heavy jacket and tossing it to the couch, Mac was determined to state his piece—dog-sledding was just too dangerous for Diana.

Diana's low husky voice floated from the kitchen. "Yes, Alex. It was really nice talking to you, too."

"Alex," Mac repeated. Alex with the smooth voice and the country-club manners. Probably had a pedigree all the way up his...

Mac's heart stopped; his fingers trembled as he forced himself to sift through the day's mail. Alex probably knew all the right moves to win a woman's heart. Mac grimaced, feeling uncomfortable in comparison. He hadn't spent much time refining his courtship abilities. Unable to stand, he sank onto the sofa, holding the mail.

"I know, Alex," Diana continued. "It is hard.... Yes, I understand.... Okay.... You, too."

Mac winced, looking at a business envelope addressed to him. He'd had Diana for a time, seen her grow and mend and laugh. And now it was time for Alex.

Mac crushed the invitation to the church social and tossed it on the table. He'd given Diana the space she needed, tried to keep his senses from being filled with her scent, her warmth.

But playing buddy to a woman he craved like a bee craved blossoms wasn't exactly the easiest thing.

When she laughed, his heart turned flip-flops.

When she sat quietly in the evenings, he felt warmed clear through.

Diana. Feminine, gentle . . . delectable and saucy.

Mac heard her come in and say, "Hi."

A woman welcoming her man.

Mac found himself trembling. Because he fought the need to tug her to him, because he needed her down to his bones, Mac kept his gaze on the mail. "Hi, yourself."

"Are we crabby?" she asked lightly, settling herself beside him.

When he glared at her, Mac suddenly discovered that Diana was wearing a transparent negligee. His eyes widened, taking in the revealing garment that had just enough beige lace to conceal some parts of her. "What in Sam Hill are you wearing?"

"I've just showered, Mac," she explained after taking a sip of tea from the cup she held in her hand. "Ms. Simpson has invited us to dinner. If you want to go, I'll change."

She crossed her legs, and Mac found himself staring helplessly at a smooth length of her thigh. He forced his eyes to her face. "That meddling old—"

"Now, Mac, that doesn't sound like you." Concerned at once, she frowned. "What is wrong?"

"Plenty. Clancy ought to be shot for teaching you anything about mushing. Okay, it's fun, I know that.

But a woman out on her own—anything could happen. What if you broke a leg? What if the dogs turned on you? Clancy's Nasty Boy weighs more than you do. What if those poachers decided to—''

"Poachers? You mean they still haven't been caught?"

Running his fingers through his hair, Mac took a deep breath. He hadn't meant to turn on her like that—it was just that he wanted her safe. She was so precious to him. "Listen, things can happen in the high country, and you wouldn't have a chance."

Diana's brown eyes darkened. "I suppose that's why you were checking up on me."

"I was checking up on a poacher sign. You just happened to be there."

"Really? Is that why you stirred up the snow with your helicopter? Hovering around like Papa Bear?"

Mac's frustration came to the boiling point quickly. "Why can't you understand, woman, that it's dangerous for you? Especially a half-pint—"

Her eyes widened incredulously. "What?"

Mac lowered his face, scowling down at her, his chin jutting out. He felt as raw as a wounded bear, wanting to strike out at something. "What kind of a screwball antic was that—making a happy face in the snow? What if you fell into a crevasse or the dogs decided to run off? You can't just pick up and leave the house to run dogs the way Clancy does, lady."

Just a fraction of an inch away from his lips, Diana asked carefully, "Why can't I, Mac? Didn't I have your permission? Who are you, the lord of my life?"

Mac framed her face with his big hands. "This is why not." Placing his mouth on hers, Mac let his savage needs erupt. Roughly he deepened the ravenous kiss. He took her tongue into his mouth, caressed it with his own and felt his body throb with the need to enter her. Mac needed to claim his woman. To show her his heart, to bind her to him.

Forcing himself to end the kiss, Mac looked down at Diana's wide-eyed expression and her swollen lips. He'd kissed her with every ounce of his hot and insistent desire. He'd shocked her, he knew, looking into her darkening eyes.

"So I'm not smooth like Alex." He ground out each word.

"No, you're not," she agreed, watching him steadily. "You never were." Her tongue flicked out to moisten her bottom lip.

Mac felt the cut straight down his chest. He'd shown her the rough side of his passion. And scared her. There wasn't a reason in the world why she'd stay with him now. Where had all his good intentions gone?

Mac felt ill. He had to escape, to lick his wounds in private. "I'm taking a shower."

In the bathroom, Mac turned on the water full force. Stripping off his clothes, he stepped into the steaming hot shower. He closed his eyes and saw Diana's pale face. She was probably packing her bags now.

He scrubbed his flesh almost viciously, wishing he hadn't grabbed her with the debonair polish of a Borneo wild man. Hell, he was wild. Wild with fear of losing Diana. To Alex or a hungry mountain cat. Or a wayward bullet from a poacher's rifle.

Or maybe just his own clumsiness. He cursed at himself for mishandling her. He'd probably shocked her right down to her bones.

Mac lifted his face to the stream of hot water. He took a deep breath and wondered if she'd send him a postcard after she cooled down.

Maybe someday she'd accept his apology.

He heard a sound and turned to see Diana's small hand pressed flat against the shower door. "Get out of there, Mac."

"You get out of here and I will," he exploded, feeling caught by frustration and need of Diana. "Isn't anything private around here?"

"Okay." She tossed a towel over the glass door, and he heard the bathroom door click shut.

He turned off water, toweling himself dry. "'Okay', she says. Just like that," he muttered, wrapping the towel around his waist. "How in the hell can you get a good fight stirred up with 'Okay'?"

When Mac jerked open the shower door, he found Diana leaning against the counter, smiling patiently. "Do you always talk to yourself in the shower?"

He glared at her, feeling raw and happy to see her. Placing his hands on his hips, Mac narrowed his eyes. "Sometimes a man has to have some privacy. Why is it females feel as though they have to pry under a man's skin?"

Diana trailed a slender finger down his damp chest, then looked up at him, her eyes dark. "You've had your privacy long enough, MacLean. Tell me what you feel."

Mac glanced at the mirror behind her, which revealed the curves of Diana's trim back. The negligee swooped almost to her shapely bottom. He swallowed, forcing himself not to think of the fascinating little dimple just at the base of— In another moment he'd be grabbing her. "Not a chance."

Her fingertips circled his nipples; she watched as they hardened. Then she stroked his cheek. "Mac, I think you're afraid of me."

He jerked his head away from her touch.

"Mac, don't make me come after you," she threatened softly. "I can do it, you know."

"What in Sam Hill are you talking about, woman?" he asked sharply, aware of his body hardening, heating at her nearness.

When she unwrapped the towel that was around his hips, Mac trembled. "You're pushing your luck," he said unsteadily, feeling genuine panic as the towel fell to the floor. If she touched him again, he'd burn, he'd explode with the need to claim her. . . .

Diana's skin was flushed, hot against his flesh as she brushed her cheek across his chest. Holding his eyes, she undressed and dropped the silken confection over his towel.

He closed his eyes. When they'd made love the very first time, he'd held back and she'd trusted him. Would he lose her now if he exposed his unrestrained passion?

When her lips nibbled his, he could feel her hunger, feel the potent beckoning. Stepping up to him,

Diana let her softness curve into the damp hard planes of his body. "Take me," she whispered against his throat.

Mac fought his blatant desire, his flesh aching to join with hers. He knew he couldn't hold back the passion that kept him riveted to the floor. If ever a man wanted to possess a woman, he was that man. His throat dry, he whispered, "No."

Diana stilled, the small hardened tips of her breasts searing his chest. She leaned back to look up at him curiously. "No?"

Mac knew he had to escape or damn himself. He sidestepped her to walk to his bedroom bureau. He jerked open a drawer, taking out a pair of neatly folded briefs only to have Diana snatch them away from him.

In the faint light of the bedside lamp, he saw Diana toss his underclothing to the bed. She crossed her arms beneath her breasts, the motion raising them. His gaze followed the gentle swell of her hips and the lines of her slender legs—a seductive view that caused Mac to perspire. He tried to force his gaze away and found the task impossible.

Frowning, she tapped her toe on the braided rug. "I won't have it, Mac. You can be ill-tempered and nasty and act like a cornered old buck deer, but I won't have you keeping anything from me. I won't live like this— with everything tucked neatly away, words left unsaid."

Her finger prodded his chest. "You've been running away since New Year's. Just what is your problem, mister?"

Suddenly his bedroom seemed small. Diana, standing in her birthday suit, her eyes flashing angrily up at him, could drive a man to the limits. "Leave me alone," he said between his teeth, glaring back at her.

Her eyebrows went up. "Oh. You've reverted to the womanless hermit stage, then."

"Watch it," he warned evenly, wanting to run his hands down her body, feel the racing of her heart against his. Lack of sleep and his desire for her had placed him on edge. He'd taken her cautiously the first time. But not now. He wouldn't be able to hold back if they made love now. And then she'd run.

Diana studied him coolly. "I guess it's up to me, then."

In the next instant, she pressed him against the wall, looping her arms around his neck. She smiled softly, and Mac's hands involuntarily fitted to her back and caressed its smoothness.

"There. I've got you. . . . Give in, Mac."

When she stood on tiptoe to kiss him, Mac lost himself. Silken skin and tempting lips drove him to the limit and pushed him over. Mac could feel the primitive hunger beat through him as her lips parted, allowing his tongue entrance. Beneath his hands, her body moved, supple and willing to meet his demands. Her thighs pressed against his, increasing the ache.

Sweeping her up into his arms, Mac carried Diana to the bed.

"Oh, Mac," she whispered urgently. Holding him tightly, Diana's fingers tangled in his hair, bringing his mouth to hers, as though she, too, had hungers that raged out of control.

Mac's hands roamed over her feverishly, demanding as they stroked the length of her. He trembled, trying to bank the consuming fires momentarily.

Then Diana thrust against him, nibbling on his earlobe. "Don't hold back, Mac. Not now."

He breathed heavily, the desire rising. Diana opened to him, urged him into her fully, and they became one body, one driving force.

He'd waited too long, the tethers leashing him cut by the softness that was Diana. For a moment he stilled, absorbing the pleasure of Diana's warmth. She trembled, moving slightly beneath him. "Take me, Mac," she whispered huskily.

And then there was no waiting, only the wild beating hunger driving them on. He could feel the throbbing deep within him, his hands caressing her breasts.

His passion burned, the flames growing higher as Diana met his demands and issued her own. The bonding, sweet and furious, tasted of eternity and promises and sharing.

Each sound she made and the sweetness of her body enclosing him urged him on. Relentlessly, he tasted her tender body, savoring the taut buds of her breasts, relishing her satin-smooth skin.

Her soft arms and legs held him to her. Her head was thrown back against the first rippling tide of heat. Her fingers tensed up on his shoulders as she gave herself fully to the sensation.

Mac felt the surging ecstasy rise in her as she met his powerful rhythm. The tempest rose, swirling inside them as Mac showed her his primitive desperation, his need of her and more.

Later, as Diana's soft breath flowed across his chest, her head resting on his shoulder, Mac was overwhelmed with love and felt his eyes burn. Tears trailed down his temple as Diana's hand smoothed his chest, her palm catching the beat of his throbbing heart.

Diana turned and propped an elbow up on his chest. She kissed his hand when he tucked a damp strand behind her ear. "I love you like this, Mac. My own snuggly bear."

She nuzzled his chest, and he savored the intimate tangle of their limbs a moment longer. "I know you're tired," she said softly, blowing into his ear. "But tell me what's wrong?"

How could he tell her of his fears? "I'm just tired."

"Like hell."

He raised his eyebrows, feeling his mouth curve into a smile. "Clancy needs to watch his language."

Diana kissed the hard corners of his mouth, and Mac began to melt again. "You're the strongest person I know, Mac. Why are you frightened?" she whispered, tracing the contours of his lips with her tongue.

He breathed lightly beneath her sensual forays, bothered by the shattering driving way he'd taken her. "Did I hurt you?"

She laughed, the sound as soft as the mountain wind caressing the columbine flowers. "You freed me. I soared." Lifting herself, Diana lay on top of him. Her eyes, soft and drowsy and mysterious, looked down at him. "I've never felt like more of a woman."

She curled her arms around him, whispering against his neck, "Stop fighting me. I'm determined to have my way with you. I love this—the whispering, the sharing. Now tell me."

Diana could feel Mac's hard body tense, as though preparing to take a blow. Lifting her head, she placed her palm against his rough cheek. His black eyes flickered, looking away almost guiltily. "I have things to work out."

"Mmm. You heard me talking with Alex, didn't you?"

Mac turned to her slowly, his expression almost flat, evasive. It was then that Diana knew how he shielded himself, drawing back, aching.... Taking his hand, she linked her smaller fingers with his. His palm was warm and safe and rough with work. She'd seen those hands run over an ill calf, searching, helping.

"Let me tell you a story," she began softly, continuing to look at their joined hands. She could feel his breath fill his chest and linger before easing slowly out. As though he had taken a sharp blow and needed time to recover.

Against the white pillowcase, Mac's rugged dark face and black hair appeared as timeless as the mountains beyond the bedroom window. A man who would endure, she thought. Beneath her, his heart pounded hard and steady.

She held him, the strength of him leashed by her light touch. "I wish Alex the best. But he's caused trouble, and I called to correct him."

"I see." Mac's long hard body shuddered; his eyes glittered beneath the long sweep of lashes. She saw the flash of pain, quickly concealed.

Diana smiled, knowing that she would pursue him if he withdrew. She'd never wanted to corner a man, but Mac was an altogether different story.

"Oh, God, I don't think I can take this," Mac muttered, watching her. "How considerate of you," he offered, easing her from him. "I don't think I've ever had such a discussion after...lovemaking."

Sensing him running away, Diana felt a cold wash of panic. Throwing caution to the wind, she reached for a pillow and plummeted him with it. "You hard-headed... I'm trying to have an intelligent conversation with you about emotions! I've had enough of your hiding, enough of being held at arm's length."

"Hey!" Catching her arms, Mac pulled her under him and pressed down on her full length.

The look she sent him back was pure sensuality, inviting. "I won't break," she whispered huskily, feeling the driving desire rising in him. "Oh, Mac..."

His mouth was warm, lingering, worshiping as he rubbed his lips across hers. "Are you telling me you need me, lady?" he asked roughly.

"Oh, Mac. I do need you so."

He brushed the pad of his thumb across her hot cheek, watching her eyes darken. "Why were you wearing that sexy slinky thing?"

She answered honestly, her heart fluttering as his lips hovered near her aching breast. "To seduce you, pure and simple."

"You've certainly accomplished the task."

"Beginner's luck, darling. Maybe we should see if my luck holds."

"Hallelujah."

Nine

Mac insisted on taking Diana to work the next morning, despite her objections. He treated her with endearing, old-fashioned, courtly manners. As though he were afraid to mishandle her, fearing she'd run away.

Watching him stand near the wood stove, talking to her boss and several other men as they sipped their coffee, Diana didn't think she could refuse him anything. Tilting her head, Diana considered Mac's easy long-legged stance. Looking very appealing in his thick cable-knit sweater and jeans, he periodically glanced toward her. Something blazed when their eyes met, a deep stirring heat that had nothing to do with the wood fire.

Diana felt her bones melt. For just the space of a breath, she felt Mac locked against her, hungry and demanding.

She felt rosy and cherished and very well loved. Mac was as rugged as the country and as open with his heart—and he was hers. Once Mac had determined she could hold her own with his passion, he wanted everything. Demanded everything. Was it possible the month was January and not spring? Was she eighteen again?

Wingman glanced her way. "Hey, Diana. How about more coffee?" he asked, raising his mug.

Mac's head turned toward her, causing her hand to tremble as she lifted the steaming pot from the brewer. Walking around the cheese barrel, Diana could feel the pull of his desire.

He was gazing at her so deeply, as though he could see through her maroon turtleneck sweater and worn jeans. She blushed right down to her toes. She liked being cherished and touched as though she were precious silk and satin. At the same time, she loved being his friend. A man like Mac was one to hold on to, and to make commitments to for forever.

Crossing to the group of standing men, Diana refilled their mugs. She wanted to turn to Mac and say, "Let's go home, darling. Show me again how much you need me...."

Instead she settled for a quiet smile up at him. The rest of the men, conversing in low rumbling voices, seemed outside their intimate loving circle. Mac took the coffeepot from her to place it on a table. Wrapping his arm around her, he drew her to his side.

It was a natural gesture to place her arm around his waist. Hooking her thumb over his leather belt, Diana leaned against him.

It was this, the sharing, that she had wanted so desperately. The comfortable loving tenderness that a man like Mac could provide.

Neil chuckled. "By the looks of things, you two lovebirds had better get married soon. The whole town is dying to throw a big shindig."

"What do you mean?" Mac's fingers tightened on Diana's upper arm.

"Rayfield's been crowing he's going to be asked to be best man, once you get wise that he purposely sent you Diana. Thought he'd done you and her a favor. Said she looked like a stray, and you were the local stray collector. He had plenty of rooms that night she blew into town. Had her room key right in front of him when he got the idea."

Wingman's grin widened. "Benevolence finally put one over on Old Mac. We were just waiting to see the sparks fly."

"I didn't know." Mac grinned slowly. "But he's invited to the chili feed Diana and I will be throwing soon. So are the rest of you."

Henry Murphy's round face lighted up. "You're kidding. I thought we'd never be invited to the almighty MacLean estate. In fact, we've all been afraid you'd mess up and she'd light out as soon as she found you out. She's not wearing a ring yet."

Diana didn't need a ring to feel her commitment to Mac. She suddenly realized that in her heart, she had already decided to spend her life loving Mac. Life included making all sorts of decisions, and sometimes the heart knew a better direction than any bundle of sensible inhibitions. Besides, she didn't intend to have him bullied into marriage.

"The little woman needs a ring of some sort, Mac," another man offered. "If she were mine, I'd be wanting to put my mark on her. Other than those cute little marks on her neck, of course."

When Mac didn't answer, Diana looked up to see him studying her closely. When his gaze ran down her throat, his expression changed sharply. He swallowed, easing his hand up her arm stealthily to tug up the neck of her sweater.

Wingman sipped his coffee, his eyes sparkling. "Look at the two of them blushing just like kids. Cute, isn't it?"

"Okay, Neil, that's enough," Mac stated sharply.

"Whoa. Just teasing, boy." Wingman winked at Diana. "Come on, men, I'll show you the new compound bows that just came in. Got some muzzle loader kits in at a fair price. When the primitive hunts come around, you'll have your muskets ready."

As soon as the men left, Mac took Diana's hand and tugged her behind a fly rod display. He traced the tiny bruises on her throat with his forefinger.

She wrapped her fingers around his wrist, feeling the steady beat of his pulse. "You only loved me, Mac."

"That I did," he murmured huskily, the intimate tone causing her to quiver deep inside. "What are we going to do about it, lady?"

Before she could answer, Wingman called over to them, "By the way, Ms. Simpson said you two stood her up last night. She had the preacher over to dinner, too. Why didn't you show up, Mac?"

Mac looked down at Diana, humor and regret in his gaze. "Looks like they're going to keep it up if I don't get out of here."

He hesitated, seeming to want to say something else, when Wingman called, "Oh, lover boy—"

"Don't lift anything heavy, honey," Mac instructed her after a brief hard kiss. "And if Clancy drops by today, tell him your sledding days are over, okay? You could get hurt."

He was gone without hearing her quiet firm answer. "No, I will not, Mac."

The early afternoon sun striking the snow-covered mountains caused Mac to squint behind his sunglasses. He kept the helicopter hovering over a snowmobile trail, following it and planning his keeping-Diana tactics.

The new trail led to a stand of trees, and Mac circled the aspens, searching for poacher signs. The snowmobiles weren't following the designated trails, and he'd already spotted a freshly killed doe.

"Okay, MacLean. You think you're up to trying again, huh? You know she could walk out at anytime, don't you?" he asked himself, swerving around a rocky butte. "She caught you flat-footed, you old goat. Got you stirred up until you forgot you were her friend. Came up on your backside. Now, what are you going to do?"

Mac checked his fuel level before continuing toward Smokey Mountain. "Okay," he continued, debating with himself as he followed the winding trails. "You haven't got a thing to hold her in Colorado. She could just be feeling gratitude."

Somehow Diana's lovemaking didn't feel like thank you's. It felt like . . . making love.

"I can design and build a modern house. I can even manage moving, if she wants to. It's just that somewhere in there, I feel as if I've taken advantage of her weakness. Women are delicate emotional creatures that way, especially Diana. Mac, you've just got to give her a little space, old boy. Keep cool while she's figuring out things." He shook his head and tightened his grip on the controls.

"Giving her space won't work," he argued with himself. "It's time to sweep her off her feet. Time to get her to say 'I do' and worry about whatever comes after, later. You're committed, son. Shoot, you know right now there will never be another woman for you. Try the champagne bit. Get down on one knee—get romantic. Tell her you love her, and you do, of course."

He caught the glint of metal and circled a thick stand of trees near an old avalanche. "Dogsledding and lifting heavy stuff is out, of course," he continued. "And walking by herself. I'll take care of her— What in Sam Hill?"

The sharp crack of a rifle shot sounded over the whirring rotor blades at the same instant that Mac spotted Terry Blakely's distinctive snowgear.

* * *

Diana pushed the huge antique dresser aside to scrub the hardwood floor beneath. She'd found Mac's note that he'd be late and thought it the perfect time to start making changes in the bedroom. She'd already done the living room yesterday.

Mac needed to make room for her in his life, she decided. Just as she had rearranged his closet to make room for her clothes, he needed to make internal adjustments, too. "Because I love the big lug doesn't mean he's setting up the rules of my life," she muttered.

Bending to tug a braided rug aside, Diana paused. "I suppose he'll do that backward slide, that sidestepping routine, when I tell him I love him. He's not an easy man to court. And I don't think I'll give him an ounce of space this time. Aggressive women may not be on his menu, but I think he can hold his own."

When Red whined, she sank to her knees and patted his head. "He's a heck of a guy, Red," she told the husky. "Caring, gentle... Okay, he's got a thing about leaving his chili seasonings alone. And he likes to play bagpipes—he could use lessons."

By the time she had scrubbed and rewaxed Mac's bedroom, Diana and Red had worked out Mac's entire problem: he was just too protective. She stood and rolled her cramped shoulders, then arranged her sons' pictures on the bureau, tracing the brass frames lovingly. She fussed over a basket of mauve silk roses and white baby's breath on a starched doily.

Diana studied the room she intended to share with Mac. The mauve curtains softened the rough-cut wall planks. A thick beige-and-dark-rose comforter covered the polished brass bed, and a light tan plush rug partially covered the beautiful hardwood floor. Before closing the door, Diana stated, "I'll leave his bagpipes and his chili alone...maybe. He might not like it, but I'm sledding to my heart's content. Clancy says I'm getting good enough to race, and I intend to."

Grinning, she bent to ruffle Red's fur. "I can't believe myself, Red. Diana Phillips—den mother, crosswalk monitor and bridge club chairman—loving a man so hard and seducing him."

Three hours later, Diana scanned the night beyond the house. When Mac worked evenings, helping the sheriff, he usually found time to circle the house. It was his way of checking on her, making sure that she hadn't slid into a snowdrift.

After another two hours, the grandfather clock clanged twelve times. Diana placed her teacup firmly on the saucer. "I'm calling the sheriff, Red."

Picking up Mac's radio handset, she pushed the button, copying his actions. "Ah, this is Diana. Could I please speak to the sheriff?"

The last of a man's rough curse shot through the radio's static before the sheriff answered. "This is 209. I'm the sheriff, kid. Get off the air quick. Just turn off the set and don't push any buttons, got it?"

Diana swallowed. She might not know radio code signals, but she had to know about Mac. She pushed the button again and spoke into the handset. "This is Diana Phillips," she enunciated clearly.

"This is Sheriff Sam Michaels. Get off the air, lady. We've got problems enough with Mac."

A cold wave of panic caused her to tremble. She clenched the hand monitor. Why hadn't she turned on the radio before? Why hadn't someone called her?

The sheriff's rough voice came over the static. "Look, just get off the air, Diana. Mac is working with the game warden and me. He's in a little trouble right now, and we're trying to get together a rescue team."

Diana's panic turned into sheer white-hot anger. "I'll get off the radio when you tell me where you're at."

"Do you know the penalty for waylaying the law, lady? Get off that thing so we men can get a team together."

Diana pushed the button grimly. "I want to know your location. I have a right to be there."

"It's snowing, there's a blizzard brewing up on Smokey now, and that's where Mac crashed, okay?" the sheriff answered hotly. "We got the violators when they came down, and we've got some radio contact with Mac. He's okay, just a broken leg and a few bruises, he thinks. Now, I know you're upset, but will you get the blue blazes off that thing?"

If Diana knew anything, she knew she was not staying put while Mac was in danger. Eventually, the sheriff—apparently coached by others—told her their location.

The moment Diana stopped the pickup in front of the group of men, Wingman jerked open the door. "Diana, you ought to have better sense than this!"

Dressed in her warmest sledding outfit, Diana leaped out into the snow. She patted her thigh, motioning for Red to follow. "Where's Mac?"

Wingman shivered in the subzero arctic wind, the snow biting his face. "Come on into the makeshift tent. There's coffee—"

The sheriff marched up to Diana. "So you got here. I thought we might have two emergencies."

Taking her arm, he led her into the canvas tent. He shoved a Styrofoam cup of coffee into her hand. "Mac went down up on Old Smokey. From what we can figure out, a high-caliber rifle helped him."

"What are you doing to rescue him?" Diana stared at the game warden's expression and was frightened by what she saw. She took a deep breath, ordering herself to calm down.

The sheriff sipped his scalding coffee, studying the snow. "It's a touchy one, Diana. The copter went down in the high country. From what Mac says, any kind of noise at all could cause an avalanche that would take off the whole face of the mountain. If we run another copter up there, it could be dangerous."

"What about snowmobiles?" she asked as Red nudged her thigh, as though seeking comfort. She buried her fingers in his pelt.

"Same thing. They make noise. And at that distance, gas and the high altitude are serious problems. Other than that, Mac's leg won't take a lot of wrestling around. Add a blizzard expected to arrive in another twenty hours, and you've got bad news."

Red whined, looking up at her. "What about a sled?"

The game warden shook his head. "Dangerous. The only skilled musher around is old Clancy. He's out of shape. He wouldn't be worth a hoot. The rest of them haven't run the high country."

"But I have. Call Clancy—get his team up here. I can do it." Diana saw the hesitation in the men's faces. "I can do it," she repeated quietly.

The sheriff was the first to explode. "Hell, no! I'm not about to let you go up. He'd be all right if we left him there a while longer. The thing is, that mountain purely likes to avalanche. Ridiculous...a half-pint female—"

Diana smiled. She would show them what this half-pint could do. "I'm going up," she stated with quiet authority.

The sheriff resisted, uttering a stream of oaths that heated the canvas tent. But in the end, he sent a man after Clancy and his dogs.

In an hour, Clancy was squatting beside a light birch sled. He had been giving Diana plenty of instructions. He rubbed snow around the lashings to freeze and strengthen them. "She's a good one," he said with pride, referring to the sled. "Built to travel fast, runs on the snow like a leaf on the wind."

He glanced up at Diana. "Scared? For Mac or yourself?"

"Both," she admitted, trying to remember the nurse's instructions about the pain pills and the first-aid wrapping for Mac's leg.

"The dogs are wanting to run, girl. They can feel it deep inside. You can do it, the same as them. Just remember, if you come to a snowbridge, take it easy.

Walk the dogs across, one at a time, if you have to—"

The sheriff stormed out of the tent. "Mac went down with two bottles of expensive Scotch. He's as drunk as a skunk and singing those damned Highland songs into the radio!"

He shot an embarrassed look at Diana. "Oh, hell, Mac made me promise to kiss you and tell you he loves you."

The sheriff—thought to be as hard as flint—bent down awkwardly to kiss her cheek. "Keep it to yourself, lady. But you're okay with me, too. Mac deserves the best."

"That she is," Clancy agreed. "Look here, me darlin'. You get up there in avalanche country, and you talk quiet to those dogs. They won't bark, then. Got it?"

The sheriff shifted uneasily, looking up at the mountain. "She's hell up there now. The only thing we've got going for us are those freak sun spots. Without them even radio transmission would be impossible."

The sheriff handed her a small radio transmitter/receiver. "Any questions on how to operate this thing? Mac's drunk, but he's giving us a chance to talk, now and then."

She nodded, then glanced up at the snow-covered mountain. It had always looked beautiful to her, but now it was only forbidding. Mac was up there, hurt, needing her. She hadn't even told him she loved him.

At the first light, Diana called to Red. The husky stood in his harness, shaking the snow from him.

Clancy's malamutes copied him. "I'm ready," Diana told the men.

"I packed you a musher's special—sticks of butter, chocolate bars and a bunch of other stuff—to eat while you run," Clancy explained. "You can do it, darlin'. Old Clancy never taught a dummy yet." He hugged her awkwardly. "I'll pray to the good Lord for your safety."

Just past the timberline, Diana could feel the power rising in the dogs. The light sled coursed over the snow as though it were polished glass.

"Push them," Diana repeated Clancy's instructions beneath her knitted face mask. "And keep strong myself." After an hour, she reached into her provisions to extract a chocolate bar. "Mac, I'm coming."

Following the sheriff's orders, she repeatedly called the emergency base. Clancy talked her through the rest stop, reminding her to feed the dogs and check the traces. "Stop playing the lady with Nasty Boy," the old timer ordered through the radio static. "Let him run his heart out."

The shadowy pines gave way to rocky buttes and startling sweeps of deep snow. Coming onto a straight stretch, Diana called the base station. "The snow is different up here, Clancy. Like ice."

"Huh," he answered. "Stop the team and put on their booties. That ice could cut their pads. Lash 'em tight and knock Nasty Boy across the muzzle if he snarls. Check the booties every so often for wear—replace 'em if you have to. I packed plenty."

Diana smiled beneath her face mask. The old man was with her every inch of the way. "I love you, Clancy."

The radio crackled. "What the hell is going on?" Mac demanded belligerently. "I thought I heard Diana's voice."

Taking a deep breath, Diana answered, "I'm coming up, Mac. I'm running the dogs straight for you. Clancy and the sheriff are directing me. You'll have to talk to me now."

"Huh?" After a moment's silence, Mac growled. "Those idiots let you take a sled up here?"

When his blistering salty opinions of the men hiding behind women's skirts ended, Diana said simply, "I love you, Mac."

The radio crackled, and Clancy singsonged, "I love you, too, Mac. The sheriff kissed your girl, and I hugged the daylights out of her. Kanoodled her nice and tight against me. What are you going to do about it?"

"Nothing," Mac responded, "but kill you. Wring your scrawny neck with my bare hands."

When Mac finished raving, the nurse's voice came across Diana's receiver. "Diana, Clancy says Mac is drunk. You can't give him those pain pills now," she said urgently.

"What do I do, instead?" Diana asked.

Mac's unsteady voice answered the question. "Easy. Let me drink whiskey until I'm blind."

"Nurse?" Diana asked.

"Okay, honey. Let him have his way."

"It's good stuff, too," Mac added. "Not like Donaldson's rotgut."

Diana crossed a shadowy pass, the snowdrifts slanting precariously on the rocky bluffs. When she described the spot, the game warden answered, "Mac should be around there someplace."

Mac continued to grumble. "Hell of a thing, to let a sweet little woman save me. She should stay put where it's safe and let the lot of you freeze your—"

The radio crackled as Diana allowed the dogs to swerve around a fallen log. It was full light now, with threatening clouds looming around the mountains. Diana's face mask caught the freezing mist, and she quickly replaced it. Clancy asked about the dogs and decided they were strong enough not to rest. "Wait 'til you find Mac, then change their booties and boil 'em some blood broth out of the pack. Take a shot or two of the whiskey yourself. You'll need it. Mac's not happy with the lot of us over this. Okay, missy?"

"Damn it, Clancy," Mac roared. "Where is she?"

Diana pressed the radio button. Mac could fuss over her later to his heart's content, but right now he needed a firm hand. "Mac, shut up. Tell me where you are."

"You're bossy. Never did like bossy women. And you changed all the furniture around. I bumped my knee—of course that's the leg that's broken. Like it was hexed or something. . . ."

"Oh, brother." The sheriff's rough voice entered the conversation. "Diana, follow that mouth."

"Mac, where are you?"

"I'm in a snow cave. Tucked in nice and tight. Wish you were here with me, honey. Hey, you guys, get off the radio, okay? Some of this stuff is personal."

Ten

───

After taking care of the dogs, Diana entered the cave.

Stretched out on a parachute covering the ground, Mac looked very pale. "Who are you? What the hell is going on?" he asked in a raw voice that was nearly a shout. "This isn't a Sunday school picnic up here, you know."

Diana straightened the blanket across the mouth of the cave, then patted the snow to secure the flap.

She turned to Mac, jerking off her parka hood and face mask. Pain etched his face, deepening the lines. His eyes flicked anxiously over her, and his hand shook as he set down a near empty whiskey bottle.

His gaze fastened on her face, then trailed across her mussed hair. "You're crazy, woman," he stated in a low raspy voice.

She saw the sheer fear in his expression before it was replaced by anger. She wanted to run to him. She was his friend and his lover; she intended to share his life.

But now wasn't the time to sort out their relationship, to end the game and make serious promises. She had to remember the nurse's instructions and follow them carefully. Mac didn't look pliant—if she had to bully him to make him take her directions, she would.

She opened a thermos of his chili, poured some into a cup and handed it to him with a spoon. "So how are you?" she asked casually.

He glared at her. "Just peachy. Getting ready for the ball. I hope you enjoyed yourself."

Seating herself on a corner of his parachute, Diana wondered how long she had loved him. It was a lasting love, fueled by passion and gentleness. Gazing at the dark stubble covering his jaw, Diana decided that Mac was more attractive than ever. "It was a nice run," she said, tilting her head to study him. She unwrapped a chocolate bar and munched on it as he glared at her. "You know, Mac, I think we'll have our pictures taken together. A nice brass frame—"

Mac stared at her. "This is no time to talk about decorating, woman! I've been worried sick about you." He paused, frowning as he chewed thoughtfully. "Something tastes different," he murmured ominously. "You've been messing with my recipe, on top of everything else."

"Mmm. Someone had to. What do you think?"

He probed the mixture with his spoon. "I think that's Donaldson's secret spice in there. What is it?"

She winked at him, grinning. Somehow, her resolution not to talk about their future together was just not going to work out. "It's my secret now. The only way I'll let you know, is if you'll share your life with me," she returned easily, looking around. "I didn't know it would be so light in here. I'd thought it would be very dark."

Mac looked as if he had swallowed ten whole red-hot chili peppers. "What are you saying?"

Diana licked her bottom lip clean of chocolate. She cautioned, "Shh. Keep your voice down, sweetheart. There's a whole ton of snow over the cave that would just love to crush us. Now could you tell me about your leg, please?"

Mac cursed under his breath, gazing toward the snow ceiling as though he were asking for heavenly guidance. "Women!"

She poured her chili into a paper cup. She reached for the whiskey, put in a measure, then stirred it in.

"What in Sam Hill are you doing now?" Mac erupted as she sampled the mixture.

"Clancy told me to take a drink. I have to eat, so I'm saving a step."

Mac's expression was undisguised disbelief. After a pause, he lifted the bottle and drank from it. Wiping the back of his hand across his mouth, he stared at her, challenging her. "We're in a hell of a mess up here, lady. And in the middle of everything, you start talking about sharing lives."

"Uh-huh. When are you going to tell me you love me, Mac?"

His face softened. "I thought you knew. If you left, you'd take my life with you. Pure and simple."

"That's nice." She turned to him fully, fierce longing blazing in her. "Say it, Mac. You've told the world—now tell me. Face-to-face."

"I love you," he said, then his expression changed to one of sadness. "I didn't want to care. Feeling is like ripping parts of you away, throwing them into oblivion. Caring is risky."

"I felt the same." She was suddenly shy. "I thought I was too old to feel this way. I really didn't want to, then along came this friend. . . . You listened and you cared, Mac. And then the other part came, too. It frightened me, wanting you so badly, the feeling of being all new."

After stripping his gloves off, Mac reached for her. He cradled her face and pulled her to him. "Come here. . . ."

She held her lips from his—waiting for him to meet her on equal terms. "All or nothing, Mac," she whispered.

He rubbed his nose against hers, smiling. "You're quite a woman. My woman."

It was there in his expression—all the fierce loving pride she'd sought for a lifetime. The warmth and the tenderness just for her, just as she was. . . . Mac brushed her lips with his, and she felt the sensual pull of him draw her nearer. "Diana the huntress," he murmured softly, drawing her hand to his mouth. His lips pressed into her small palm as he closed his eyes.

He held her hand there, silently making his promises. Then he opened his eyes and looked longingly at her. "Does wonders for a man's ego—your coming after me."

"I always will," she returned, kissing him. "Count on it."

"We'll melt this cave if we keep this up," he whispered rawly a moment later.

Forcing herself away, Diana lifted the parachute material covering his legs. Mac had formed a rough splint using a branch and tied it to his broken leg. "It's okay," he muttered, running his fingers through her hair. He watched the strands fall from his fingers. "Do you know how I feel when we make love?"

Diana zipped up his parka, pulling it tightly around his ashen face, then eased him gently to his feet. His grimace of pain caused her stomach to knot. Wrapping her arm around his waist, she led him to the sled. "Tell me, Mac. Talk to me."

Mac grunted in pain as he lowered himself into the sled. "I love you, kid," he stated roughly. Then he glanced at the low threatening clouds. "If you don't mind, honey, I think we'd better make a run for it. Please?"

When she covered him with the heavy down sleeping bag, Mac groaned weakly. "Oh, God, I think I'm going to pass out.... What are we going to do now?"

Diana leaned down to kiss his cold lips. She kissed his closed lids and the top of his nose. "Why, honey, you're going to let me take care of you. You just settle down and enjoy the ride."

"Huh?" Mac asked, gazing at her blankly. "But I'm supposed to take care of you...." Then he fainted.

* * *

Mac stirred in the warmth of his own bed, finding Diana's small body curled around his back. When he moved slightly, her bare breasts rubbed against him enticingly. Her arm draped across his waist.

From downstairs came a voice as rough as nails scratching a blackboard; Clancy sang a musher's song at the top of his lungs.

Mac held his breath, fought his throbbing headache and forced open one eye. The early light of the cloudy dawn blinded him, searing through the ruffled curtains straight on a path to the back of his head. He clamped his lips closed, feeling the softness of Diana's thighs tangle with his. Her fingers stirred and played with the hair on his chest as she rubbed his back with her cheek.

"Sweetheart?" she asked in a tone husky with sleep. "How are you feeling?"

Clancy roared, "Boyo, boyo run your dogs till their tongues drag in the snow, and you still won't beat my merry crew!"

Ray, Ms. Simpson and Donaldson joined him for the next chorus, and Mac groaned. Halting her seeking fingers by covering them with his hand, he managed to say raggedly, "I'm fine. What's going on?"

She yawned, then propped herself up on his chest. She nuzzled his neck. "How's your leg?"

"Just great, considering it's broken." He felt himself growing heated as he looked straight into Diana's drowsy eyes—just as he did every time he looked at her. He brushed a strand of hair back from her cheek and kissed her waiting lips gently.

Diana sighed, resting her cheek upon his chest. She draped a slender arm around his neck and caressed him. "I like this—waking up as Mrs. Mac MacLean, honey," she whispered.

Her hand on him felt so good, Mac thought, stroking her hair. His hand slid down her smooth back. With his other hand, he rubbed his jaw—and was surprised. "It takes me two days to grow a beard like this. What day is it?"

"It's two days later," Diana answered, then kissed his shoulder.

Suddenly, Mac's brain registered what she'd said earlier, "Mrs. Mac MacLean?"

She nibbled his tanned shoulder. "Umm. You were absolutely horrible, threatening Clancy's life. It was the least I could do."

Closing his eyes, Mac remembered the explosion of happiness that had swept through him when Diana had whispered, "Of course, I'll marry you, honey. Just let the doctor finish the cast. The sheriff can get us the license and fetch the minister. And we can take the blood test right here in the hospital."

"Now," he had demanded roughly, catching her hand to press it to his lips.

"I pronounce you man and wife," the minister had proudly proclaimed later.

Now, Mac sat up in bed. "This is no good," he stated aloud. "You shouldn't have married me just because you felt sorry for me."

Diana sat up also, sunlight caressing the uncovered curves of her body. Frowning, she tilted her head a little to the side, a gesture he knew signified a chal-

lenge. She'd done that a lot lately, challenged him.
And he'd liked it!

His gaze wandered downward to that tiny mole just
to the right of her—he looked up, trying to keep from
getting distracted. "Cover up. I can't think when
you're—like that. You make me go all haywire. I can't
think about anything but—" He tugged the sheet up,
expecting her to hold it.

Diana let the sheet fall, and he forced himself to
continue, "Besides, that crew downstairs could burst
into this room anytime. Someone ought to scrub
Clancy's mouth. Those songs aren't fit for a lady to
hear."

"They're celebrating winning the game. By the way,
Ray says I'm worth at least that antique musket, too.
I've already told Rick and Blaine about the marriage,
and they were very happy. They hinted at spending the
whole summer with us," she said, grinning.

"We're supposed to be in our honeymoon suite, my
darling husband. We have all the privacy we want,
with dinner awaiting us at the tug of that rope." She
nodded toward a cord tied to the bed.

Dazed, Mac looked around the newly decorated
room. He shook his head. "No. This won't do at all.
I had big plans—"

"It was the best we could do on such short notice.
What other plans did you have, Mac?" Diana asked
quietly.

Mac sighed. "I wanted to . . ."

"Yes?" Diana's sweet breath brushed his chest, and
Mac could feel himself melting.

"Well, I wanted to...sweep you off your feet. Anyway, I won't hold you to promises made under duress." He had to look at her just once more before she escaped....

Diana brought his hand to her mouth, ran the tip of her tongue across his callused palm. "Don't fight me, darling. I'm holding the secret chili spice as my edge." She placed his hand upon her breast, and her inquisitive fingertips began tracing his ear, then moved down his shoulder and lower. "From stray to friend to loving wife," she whispered, her lips brushing his cheek. "It's true, then, Humpty can be put together again."

Her lashes fluttered against his warm cheek playfully. "Is your leg hurting...too badly?"

Mac wriggled his toes, breathing in her sweet scent. "I am...okay."

Seating herself on his lap, Diana gently tugged his lobe with her teeth. "You're awake now, aren't you, Mac? Fully awake?"

She felt so right in his arms. Stroking her thigh, Mac agreed with a nod of his head. "You risked your life for me. I was damned proud of you."

"I love you, Mac. It's as simple as that."

He looked into her clear brown eyes and saw his future, his happiness. With Diana there would be nothing but sunlight and roses.

"I wanted to marry you, Mac—I'd already decided before your accident. I just saw my opportunity then and reached out for it." She ran her fingers through his hair, watching the black strands catch the soft light. "I've been thinking about racing sleds and learning to fly your helicopter."

"Mmm?" Mac was too distracted by her mouth to hear her last sentence. He nibbled her lips, then trailed light kisses down to her throat.

"You didn't marry me just to get the secret spice, did you?" she murmured, caressing his cheeks.

Mac's head came up, and he saw Diana's seductive smile. It took his breath away. "I love you. I've waited a lifetime for you. Let me show you why I married you."

How could a woman say no? Diana asked herself when their lips met.

* * * * *

Silhouette Special Edition

presents

★ LOVE AND GLORY ★

from
Lindsay McKenna

Introducing a gripping new series celebrating our men—and women—in uniform. Meet the Trayherns, a military family as proud and colorful as the American flag, a family fighting the shadow of dishonor, a family determined to triumph—with **LOVE AND GLORY!**

June: **A QUESTION OF HONOR** (SE #529) leads the fast-paced excitement. When Coast Guard officer Noah Trayhern offers Kit Anderson a safe house, he unwittingly endangers his own guarded emotions.

July: **NO SURRENDER** (SE #535) Navy pilot Alyssa Trayhern's assignment with arrogant jet jockey Clay Cantrell threatens her career—and her heart—with a crash landing!

August: **RETURN OF A HERO** (SE #541) Strike up the band to welcome home a man whose top-secret reappearance will make headline news . . . with a delicate, daring woman by his side.

Coming in July from

Silhouette Desire®

ODD MAN OUT #505
by Lass Small

*Roberta Lambert is too busy with her job to notice that her
new apartment-mate is a strong, desirable man. But Graham
Rawlins has ways of getting her undivided attention....*

Roberta is one of five fascinating Lambert sisters. She is as
enticing as each one of her three sisters, whose stories you have
already enjoyed or will want to read:

- Hillary in GOLDILOCKS AND THE BEHR (Desire #437)
- Tate in HIDE AND SEEK (Desire #453)
- Georgina in RED ROVER (Desire #491)

Watch for Book IV of Lass Small's terrific miniseries and read
Fredricka's story in TAGGED (Desire #528) coming in
October.

"GIVE YOUR HEART TO SILHOUETTE" SWEEPSTAKES
OFFICIAL RULES

NO PURCHASE NECESSARY TO ENTER OR RECEIVE A PRIZE

1. To enter and join the Silhouette Reader Service, rub off the concealment device on all game tickets. This will reveal the potential value for each Sweepstakes entry number and the number of free book(s) you will receive. Accepting the free book(s) will automatically entitle you to also receive a free bonus gift. If you do not wish to take advantage of our introduction to the Silhouette Reader Service but wish to enter the Sweepstakes only, rub off the concealment device on tickets #1-3 only. To enter, return your entire sheet of tickets. Incomplete and/or inaccurate entries are not eligible for that section or section (s) of prizes. Not responsible for mutilated or unreadable entries or inadvertent printing errors. Mechanically reproduced entries are null and void.

2. Either way, your Sweepstakes numbers will be compared against the list of winning numbers generated at random by computer. In the event that all prizes are not claimed, random drawings will be made from all entries received from all presentations to award all unclaimed prizes. All cash prizes are payable in U.S. funds. This is in addition to any free, surprise or mystery gifts that might be offered. The following prizes are awarded in this sweepstakes:

(1)	*Grand Prize	$1,000,000	Annuity
(1)	First Prize	$35,000	
(1)	Second Prize	$10,000	
(3)	Third Prize	$5,000	
(10)	Fourth Prize	$1,000	
(25)	Fifth Prize	$500	
(5000)	Sixth Prize	$5	

   *The Grand Prize is payable through a $1,000,000 annuity. Winner may elect to receive $25,000 a year for 40 years, totaling up to $1,000,000 without interest, or $350,000 in one cash payment. Winners selected will receive the prizes offered in the Sweepstakes promotion they receive.
   Entrants may cancel the Reader Service privileges at any time without cost or obligation to buy (see details in center insert card).

3. Versions of this Sweepstakes with different graphics may be offered in other mailings or at retail outlets by Torstar Corp. and its affiliates. This promotion is being conducted under the supervision of Marden-Kane, Inc., an independent judging organization. By entering this Sweepstakes, each entrant accepts and agrees to be bound by these rules and the decisions of the judges, which shall be final and binding. Odds of winning are dependent upon the total number of entries received. Taxes, if any, are the sole responsibility of the winners. Prizes are nontransferable. All entries must be received by March 31, 1990. The drawing will take place on April 30, 1990, at the offices of Marden-Kane, Inc., Lake Success, N.Y.

4. This offer is open to residents of the U.S., Great Britain and Canada, 18 years or older, except employees of Torstar Corp., its affiliates, and subsidiaries, Marden-Kane, Inc. and all other agencies and persons connected with conducting this Sweepstakes. All federal, state and local laws apply. Void wherever prohibited or restricted by law.

5. Winners will be notified by mail and may be required to execute an affidavit of eligibility and release that must be returned within 14 days after notification. Canadian winners will be required to answer a skill-testing question. Winners consent to the use of their name, photograph and/or likeness for advertising and publicity in conjunction with this and similar promotions without additional compensation. One prize per family or household.

6. For a list of our most current major prizewinners, send a stamped, self-addressed envelope to: WINNERS LIST, c/o MARDEN-KANE, INC., P.O. BOX 701, SAYREVILLE, N.J. 08871

If Sweepstakes entry form is missing, please print your name and address on a 3" × 5" piece of plain paper and send to

In the U.S.	In Canada
Sweepstakes Entry	Sweepstakes Entry
901 Fuhrmann Blvd	P.O. Box 609
P.O. Box 1867	Fort Erie, Ontario
Buffalo, NY 14269-1867	L2A 5X3

LTY-S69R

You'll flip . . . your pages won't!
Read paperbacks *hands-free* with

Book Mate • I

The perfect "mate" for all your romance paperbacks
Traveling • Vacationing • At Work • In Bed • Studying
• Cooking • Eating

Perfect size for all standard paperbacks, this wonderful invention makes reading a pure pleasure! Ingenious design holds paperback books OPEN and FLAT so even wind can't ruffle pages — leaves your hands free to do other things. Reinforced, wipe-clean vinyl-covered holder flexes to let you turn pages without undoing the strap . . . supports paperbacks so well, they have the strength of hardcovers!

Pages turn WITHOUT opening the strap.

SEE-THROUGH STRAP

Reinforced back stays flat.

Built in bookmark.

BOOK MARK

BACK COVER HOLDING STRIP

10" x 7¼", opened.
Snaps closed for easy carrying, too.

 **Silhouette Desire** ®

COMING NEXT MONTH

#505 ODD MAN OUT—Lass Small
July's *Man of the Month*, Graham Rawlins, was undeniably
attractive, but Roberta Lambert seemed uninterested. However,
Graham was very determined, and she found he'd do almost
anything to get her attention....

#506 THE PIRATE O'KEEFE—Helen R. Myers
Doctor Laura Connell was intrigued by the injured man washed
up on her beach. When she discovered his true identity it was too
late—she'd fallen for the pirate O'Keefe.

#507 A WILDER NAME—Laura Leone
Luke Swain was positively the most irritating man Nina
Gnagnarelli had ever met. He'd insulted her wardrobe, her
integrity and her manners. He'd also set her heart on fire!

#508 BLIND JUSTICE—Cathryn Clare
As far as Lily Martineau was concerned, successful corporate
lawyer Matt Malone was already married—to his job. Matt
pleaded guilty as charged, then demanded a retrial.

#509 ETERNALLY EVE—Ashley Summers
Nate Wright had left Eve Sheridan with a broken heart. Now he
seemed to have no memory of her—but it was a night Eve would
never forget!

#510 MAGIC TOUCH—Noelle Berry McCue
One magic night with a handsome stranger made Caroline
Barclay feel irresistible. But she didn't believe in fairy tales until
James Mitchel walked back into her life—as her new boss.

AVAILABLE NOW:

1989
IS THE YEAR
OF THE MAN!

What makes a romance? A special man, of course, and Silhouette Desire celebrates that fact with *twelve* of them! From Mr. January to Mr. December, every month has a tribute to the Silhouette Desire hero—our **MAN OF THE MONTH!**

Sexy, macho, charming, irritating . . . irresistible! Nothing can stop these men from sweeping you away. Created by some of your favorite authors, each man is custom-made for pleasure—*reading* pleasure—so don't miss a single one.

Mr. July is Graham Rawlins in ODD MAN OUT by Lass Small
Mr. August is Jeremy Kincaid in MOUNTAIN MAN by Joyce Thies
Mr. September is Clement Cornelius Barto in BEGINNER'S LUCK by Dixie Browning
Mr. October is James Branigan in BRANIGAN'S TOUCH by Leslie Davis Guccione
Mr. November is Shiloh Butler in SHILOH'S PROMISE by BJ James
Mr. December is Tad Jackson in WILDERNESS CHILD by Ann Major

So get out there and find your man!

Silhouette Desire's

MAN OF THE MONTH . . .

MOM-1R